The Hijack Adventure

The Hijack Adventure
by
Chris Wright

ISBN: 978-1-5203448-0-5

Also available as an eBook ISBN: 978-0-9954549-6-5

Website: www.whitetreepublishing.com
More books by Chris Wright on
www.rocky-island.com
Email: wtpbristol@gmail.com

The Hijack Adventure is a work of fiction. Names, characters, places, and incidents are the product of the author's imagination or are used fictitiously.

(See also www.youversion.com for free downloads of over a thousand Bible translations in over a thousand languages on your phone, tablet, and computer.)

Published by
White Tree Publishing
Bristol
UNITED KINGDOM

A Word from the Author

I first wrote this story some years ago, and things have now changed a lot, especially with electronics and digital communication. No mobile (cell) phones, digital cameras, tablets and computers back then. So although the main story is unchanged, some things have been updated to make the adventure happen today.

The word *truck*, like many other American terms, is being used more and more in Britain to describe what the British have traditionally called a *lorry*. In America, a lorry is a very large vehicle for transporting timber or heavy machinery. All very confusing! Although this story takes place in England, I'm calling British lorries *trucks*!

Other things to note: In America a mother is a mom, while over on Anna's side of the Atlantic a mother is a mum. Fathers are usually known as dad on both sides. And trainers are what Americans call sneakers. There are a few other differences, especially in the way some words are spelt. This book uses the British English spelling because that's where the adventure takes place.

Chris Wright

Measurements

The measurements in this book are in miles, feet and inches. Here is an approximate table of conversion to metric.

1 mile is 1.6km

1 yard is a little less than 1m

I hope this helps!

Chapters

Chapter One

THE OLD BARN CAFE

It was Friday, the first day of the summer holidays, and Anna Collins was on her own. She sat on a large stone in front of the Old Barn Café and watched truck after truck drive past without even slowing down for a look. If only one of them would stop, that would please her mum.

Anna was worried that their café was empty. Her mother had worked hard over the past month since moving here from the city. Anna shook her head. When she'd first been told she was moving here, she'd been excited.

The Old Barn Café had seemed such a wonderful place. It must be years and years old. Right out in the countryside, this large stone barn had been converted into a transport café for truck drivers. And now it was hers. Well, hers and her mum's.

It was these truck drivers who should be in it now. The trouble was, the place was empty. "Give a dog a bad name," Anna heard one driver say about the place. That hadn't made much sense to her at the time. She frowned now as she thought about it.

The café seemed to have a bad name with truck drivers. The people who'd run it before had been rotten cooks, and rude with it. Not like her mum. *She* was ever so good. If only the drivers could somehow find out just how good!

A noisy truck was coming along the road now. Quite slowly. Perhaps the driver was getting ready to stop. It was coming in jumpy movements. Slower and slower it came.

Anna held her breath. Then, "Please stop," she said over and over again. "Please stop. Please come in, whoever you are!"

The truck lurched to a halt right by the stone where she was sitting. The driver leaned from his cab. "How far to the nearest garage, miss?"

"I ... I don't know." Anna was suddenly lost for words. She'd been so sure the driver was going to ask about the food and....

"I can't get a signal here on my phone. Do you know if they've got a phone in the café I could use?"

"Yes."

"Inside is it?"

"Yes."

"All right if I use it?"

"Yes. Please don't go away."

The driver laughed. "Not much danger of that. This truck won't go much further today."

"Would you ... would you like a meal?"

The driver shook his head.

"Cup of tea?"

The driver shrugged his shoulders. "Could do, I suppose." He sounded impatient. "It's the phone I want, really."

"Will it go?" she asked, pointing to the truck.

The driver nodded, and restarted the engine. It sounded very uneven and not at all healthy.

Anna pointed to the truck area. "Then you'd better drive in and park. I'll go and tell Mum you're here. It's a payphone. You'll need change. And there's free wi-fi."

There was a public phone box about a mile down the road, but she wanted to get the driver inside the café. That way, he might order a meal, especially if he met her mum and could see how nice she was.

Anna ran inside. Her mother was reading the paper. The few lunch things had been cleared away. There might be a couple of trucks stopping in the early evening, but right now business was always slow. Mrs. Collins glanced up. Anna thought how tired she looked. She'd never looked like this in the city. It must be worry. It certainly wasn't overwork!

"Was that a truck I heard, Anna?"

Anna's eyes sparkled in excitement. "Yes, and he's broken down. He wants to use the phone in the cafe. I've told him he'll have to promise to eat and eat, and promise to tell all his friends about the place. I said he couldn't use the phone unless he did!"

Mrs. Collins put her arm around her daughter and squeezed her tightly. She laughed. "I wouldn't put it past you. You're a terror, you are!"

Anna smiled and felt comfortable. "I didn't really say it, but I expect he's ever such a well-known truck driver. So he'll tell all his friends and *make* them come. Then you'll be so busy you'll have to take on extra help. That means we'll have to build a larger place."

"Okay to use the phone, Ma?" The driver looked round the door. Joined to the back of the café was the small bungalow where Anna and her mother lived. "I can't get a signal on my phone."

Mrs. Collins stood up quickly. "No one can. One day I suppose someone will put a mast up. It's a payphone for customers, so you're welcome to use it. Would you like some tea?"

"Just a cuppa, thanks, Ma."

Mrs. Collins beckoned to Anna to go with her, while the driver used the phone. "You can make him his tea, Anna," she said. "Try and persuade him to have a cooked meal at the same time!"

Anna giggled. "You're as bad as I am, Mum. Let's hope he's broken down for ever so long, and then he'll *have* to eat here, or starve to death!"

She tipped some milk into a white mug while she waited for the kettle to boil. It was much quicker than waiting for the large urn to heat up.

Some of the mugs were chipped, but she'd specially chosen one of the better ones.

When her mother had taken on the Old Barn Café, all the crockery, tables, chairs, cooking utensils and "goodwill" had come with it. The "goodwill" was supposed to be the benefit of having lots of happy customers who knew the place already. The trouble was, her mother found out too late that she'd taken on "badwill". The people who'd run the café before had served terrible food.

It seemed that the place was on a drivers' unofficial blacklist, and they did their best to avoid it. Car drivers rarely stopped because there was a large sign that said TRANSPORT CAFE. Anna would have taken the sign down, but her mother wanted the place just for truck drivers. Anna's father had been a truck driver, but he'd died four years ago. It had just been Anna and her mum for what seemed like a very long time.

The driver made his call and sat down at a table. He looked slowly round at the paint on the walls. Anna wished and wished they could afford to have the whole place redecorated. The tables and chairs were old. The floor covering wasn't too bad. If they had more trade they could afford to get these things done, but until the place was smartened up a bit they were unlikely to get more trade. Her mum had said it was a sort of chicken and egg situation, whatever that meant.

"Tea ready?"

Anna brought it across for the driver. There was sugar on the tables. Nice clean piles of white sugar in clean glass bowls. Anna's mum was keen to show how well she was going to look after the customers, even if the place needed a fresh coat of paint.

"Thanks, miss. You've not been here long, have you?"

"Three or four weeks," Anna said. "Four, I think."

"Your place now?"

"My mum's."

"What happened to the last lot?"

"Dunno. We bought it when they left."

"Like it here?"

"*I* do. Mum could do with more trucks stopping. She cooks ever such *good food.*" Anna knew she was dropping a very obvious hint to the driver. "She does, honest. *Ever* such good food!"

The driver smiled. He was holding the large white mug tightly in both hands. "This tastes okay. What have you got to eat?" Then he added quickly, "I don't want much, mind."

Anna brought him a handwritten list of meals and prices. It was inside a clear plastic cover to protect it from greasy fingers. "All the food is good. You'll love it, whatever you choose," she said hopefully, wishing for all she was worth that the man would order a full meal.

"Eggs and bacon sounds good, miss. Oh, and some bread and butter."

Since opening, there had not been many drivers stopping. Of the few that had, most ordered food that Anna always thought of as breakfast.

"I'll tell my mum." She left the driver at his table. Before coming to the café she'd secretly wanted to wear a black dress and white apron like the waitresses in the restaurant in a large store she'd been to in the city. She laughed to herself now. How silly she'd look in the Old Barn Café dressed up like that!

"He's going to be here for *ages*," Anna whispered in the kitchen as she passed on the driver's order.

"Get me two eggs from the fridge. Then you can butter up a couple of rounds of bread. Has he parked near the entrance?"

Anna frowned. "I think so. Does it matter?"

Mrs. Collins winked at her daughter. "You've got a lot to learn from this business, my girl. Make sure the trucks park where they can be seen. Then other drivers will spot them and come in. No one likes coming into an empty transport café. Leastways, that's what your father always said. He went into enough. The drivers get suspicious if no one's already in there."

Anna wished she could remember more about her father. He would be away for days, driving long distance trucks all over the country, often going abroad for a week or more at a time. It was nice to have had a father who did an exciting job. But, Anna sighed to herself, how she wished he was alive today. He'd been killed in an accident while driving his truck. Her mother had never wanted to talk to her about the accident or even about her father, and she'd immediately stopped taking her to church. Suddenly life had been so different. Now, her mum was changing again, and offering to help all truck drivers by providing them with food and a short break on their journeys. Not that many seemed to want to come in. Sometimes only two or three a day.

"The eggs please, dreamy."

Anna handed two eggs to her mother. "Mum, why don't we go to church anymore?" She'd never thought to ask that question before.

Mrs. Collins shook her head. "It was your father who was so keen on going. Still, if you want to go, I'll take you to the local church or chapel at Christmas. You can choose"

To Anna, Christmas was so far away that she might as well have been told she would never go.

At that moment there came the sound of a truck manoeuvring in the park outside. Anna ran to the window. "He's leaving before he gets his meal!" she cried. "No he's not, it's another truck. Quick, Mum, come and see."

Mother and daughter looked excitedly through the small kitchen window.

"Get some burgers out of the freezer, Mum. I'll go and persuade the driver to——. Oh, here comes another truck. Two men in it. I'm ever so glad. This is going to be our lucky day. From now on, nothing will ever go wrong again!

Chapter Two

THE WRECKED CARAVAN

Earlier that day, far from the Old Barn Café, Matthew Kemp knew it was *his* lucky day. The first day of his holidays, and going straight off with his parents in their caravan. He too, thought nothing could ever go wrong.

"Matthew," his father called, "go and get Chip, and we'll be away."

He was glad Chip was allowed to come. There'd been talk of putting him into kennels. Chip came as soon as he was called, bounding along, his long tail wagging wildly behind.

Chip seemed relieved to be going in the car, and not the caravan. He never seemed to settle in the caravan, so at night he had to sleep in the car when the Kemp family were safely tucked up for the night. Matthew had no idea what sort of dog Chip was, but someone said he had a bit of retriever in him. He was quite tall, thin, pale fawn, with short hair that was always coming out on the carpets and furniture. To Matthew he was precious, and not just any old dog. He was Chip, and Matthew Kemp had owned him for five years now.

"Come on, you two, settle down in the back." Matthew's mother turned round and smiled. "It's a good many hours till we get to the seaside. Try and get Chip to lie on the floor and perhaps he'll sleep most of the way."

Matthew tried to push Chip down and persuade him to sleep. But Chip, like his owner, was too excited to want to close his eyes. Every stretch of road, every hill and corner, brought new bits of countryside into view. And Matthew knew that every new bit of countryside meant they were just a little closer to the sea.

It was exciting to be going away, and nothing had gone wrong. Before a holiday, Matthew always started to worry that he, or one of his parents, might be ill. That had happened one year. Of course, with a caravan you could always go away on another week. It wasn't like booking up at a hotel.

<><><>

Matthew lay back and closed his eyes. He was feeling rather sleepy now. They seemed to have been going for a very long time. They would probably be stopping soon for something to eat.

Chip was on the floor at last. Matthew was very nearly asleep. Suddenly there was a loud bang, the car swerved, and Matthew heard his father shout, "Get your heads down and hold tight. *We're going to have an accident!*"

<><><>

Anna put her head out of the kitchen door to count just how many trucks there were in the park. Four. It looked as though they could be in for a rush!

There was the sound of a deep thud from further along the road, followed by loud scraping and bumping noises. Then silence.

Two men leaped down from a truck that had just arrived. Anna ran with them to the main road. Something white that looked like a large van was lying across the bend about two hundred yards up the slight hill beyond the Old Barn Café.

"Looks like a caravan to me," one of the men said to his mate.

The noise had been so loud that all the drivers and Anna's mother had now come out to see what had happened.

"Better hurry and help them," one said, and they all ran up the road.

"You stay here with me, Anna."

"But, Mum...."

"No, love. I don't want you seeing a nasty accident. Someone might be badly hurt."

"But they might need help," Anna protested, although she couldn't think how she could help. If there was wreckage to move, the strong truck drivers would be able to do it. They'd probably helped at accidents before, and knew exactly what to do.

"We'll make plenty of tea," Mrs. Collins said.

"They might be only shaken and not badly hurt, whoever they are. Some poor souls on holiday, more than likely."

One of the men came running back. "We need to use the phone again, Ma. None of us here can get a signal." It was the driver with the broken down truck who had used the phone earlier.

"Is it a *terrible* accident?" Anna asked.

"A family on a holiday with their caravan. Wrecked it is. Split wide open."

"Who are you going to phone?" Anna asked. "The ambulance?" Her heart felt to be in her mouth. It was surely bad enough to be in an accident, but to be in one when on holiday was just horrible.

"I'll ask for an ambulance just in case, but we really need to get the police and a breakdown crew to help clear the wreckage. My mates up there will control the traffic until they come."

Anna found herself holding tightly to her mother's arm while the driver phoned for help.

The man put the phone down. "I'll get back there now. Could the girl come along with some tea, Ma? They all seem a bit shaken up. There's a man and his wife, and a boy in the car." The driver nodded towards Anna. "About your age, I'd say."

Mrs. Collins told the man to wait a minute, and disappeared into the kitchen. In less than a minute she emerged with an enormous tray covered with a white cloth. "Here it is. I thought it might be needed. It's rather heavy, so it would be best if you carried it. Anna can go as well if she likes, as long as there's no blood. She might be company for that poor boy. Oh, and tell them to take plenty of sugar in the tea!"

Anna smiled. She knew that under that white cloth would two large white jugs of tea and a lot of white china mugs. Her Mother always made tea in large white jugs. And there would be one of their glass bowls piled high with sugar.

Anna hurried with the truck driver as he returned to the scene of the accident. In spite of the heavy tray, he kept getting ahead, and Anna had to run at times to keep up.

The road looked crowded. Several car drivers had stopped to see if they could help. The truck drivers were waving them on. Half the road appeared to be blocked by the wrecked caravan which was lying on its side.

"Keep well in," one of the men warned her. "Some of these drivers don't even bother to slow down as they come round that bend. They only think of themselves. They're in too much of a hurry to bother about anyone else. Wouldn't surprise me if there's another accident here soon."

But Anna hardly heard. She'd reached the caravan by now. The car that had been pulling it was parked on the grass verge. The caravan must have broken loose as it tipped onto its side, leaving the car undamaged apart from a twisted tow bar.

The front of the caravan was stuck fast in the grass bank. One side had been ripped open. Anna looked first at the caravan and then at the family sitting white-faced in their car. The truck driver was pouring them some tea, but they just sat huddled together, staring out at the road.

Anna could have wept. It seemed so horrible. A caravan was like a home, and here it was lying torn open for everyone to see inside. Knives, forks, broken plates, tins of food and clothing lay scattered along the road. No one was bothering to pick anything up. Anna wanted to cover all these things from the sight of the people who peered from their cars as they drove by. Some people even laughed, and Anna, her eyes now filled with tears, wished somehow that this had happened to her, and not to this family.

She felt a hand on her shoulder. “Awful, isn’t it?” a voice said. It was the driver who’d fetched the tea. “Come and see the family. They want to say thank you.”

Anna had to be led to the car. Her legs felt slow and heavy. She tried to smile.

A woman wearing blue jeans and a red blouse got out of the car and beckoned gently. “Thanks for coming. Tell your mum it’s lovely tea.”

“You must come and meet my mum,” Anna

heard herself saying. "You can have some more tea back at the café. And something to eat if you like. Mum won't charge you for it, I'm sure. We've got some lovely food, but ... oh, I don't expect you'll want anything to eat for a bit."

"You're a kind girl, and thank you," the woman said.

The man turned to his wife. "Why don't you and Matthew go back to the café with this girl? You both ought to get away from it all. I'll deal with everything when the police and the breakdown truck get here. I can always send for you if I need you."

"I'll take you back," Anna said. "You can come to our bungalow. That's a better place to sit than the café. It's all joined together really, but there aren't any armchairs in the café. And I'm sure Mum will let you use our private phone."

"Sounds a good offer to me," the man said. "Go on, love, go with the girl. And you as well, Matthew. By the way, we're the Kemp family. This is our son Matthew."

The driver who had brought the tray said he'd walk back with them.

"Is this the end of our holiday?" Matthew asked his mother.

"I should think so, dear. I don't suppose our caravan could be mended for weeks." Then she added after having a look at it again, "If ever."

"Are you on your way home?" Anna asked.

Matthew's mother held tightly onto Anna's hand. "It was our first day," she said, "and it looks like it's the last day for this holiday. But still, there'll be plenty of other holidays," she added brightly.

Anna would have squeezed the woman's hand even more tightly if she'd dared. How could this woman, so soon after the accident, be thinking of another holiday? But that was how she would like to be. Never put off by anything that happened to her. Always bobbing up like a cork in water. Never down for long.

Anna's mum came out to meet them, and Anna told her of the accident and how Matthew and his mum needed to sit down quietly in the bungalow.

"And, Mum," Anna said, "there are ever so many people out there. You'd better get ready for all of them. There'll be the police as well soon. And the breakdown crew. Supposing they all come back here? You look after Matthew and his mum. I'd better get some tables laid for them, and put plenty more hot water on for tea!"

Chapter Three

WHERE'S CHIP?

It was over an hour before the police and the breakdown truck finished with the wrecked caravan. An ambulance had also turned up, but left after the crew had taken a look at Matthew and his parents and found no injuries,

Matthew Kemp and his mother had done little more than sit silently with Anna's mum. The accident had given them a bad fright. Anna came to sit with them.

Suddenly Matthew jumped up. "Chip!" he shouted. "Where's Chip?"

Anna, who was staring out of the window, jumped in fright. "Who's Chip?" she asked.

Mrs. Kemp got slowly from her seat. "He'll be with your father in the car, Matthew."

"Who *is* Chip?" Anna asked again. "Your brother?"

Matthew smiled, and all of a sudden the atmosphere of the room changed. Matthew, and then his mother, began to laugh. Anna didn't mind. They seemed such kind people, and not really laughing at her at all.

"Your sister then?" Anna asked, thinking Chip was a strange sort of name for either a boy or a girl.

"My dog," Matthew said. "Come on, I'll take you to see him."

Mrs. Kemp was looking out of the bungalow window. "Yes, go on out if you like. There's your father driving into the yard now, so at least our car is still working. And here's the breakdown truck coming with the remains of our caravan. My, it does look in a sorry state."

Anna let out a gasp of horror. The caravan lurched and wobbled as it was towed into the truck park, with one of the breakdown men walking behind to pick up the pieces that dropped into the road.

"This is my dad," Matthew said to Anna, as they ran out. "Dad, this is Anna. She lives here. How's Chip?"

"Chip? I thought he was with you. I've not seen him since...."

"Dad! Oh, Dad! He's lost! He's run away in a strange place. He'll never know where to find us. Never, never, *never*!"

Mr. Kemp got wearily out of his car. "Go and give him a call. But be careful of the traffic," he warned. "Now, where's your mother?"

Matthew explained about the bungalow behind the café. At this moment Mrs. Collins came out and called to her daughter. "Anna love, come and give me a hand. All these men want tea and something to eat."

"All right, Mum." Anna turned to Matthew. "I hope you find Chip. I'll come out and help you as soon as I can."

"Can I give you a hand with the tea?" Mr. Kemp asked.

"Bless you, no," Mrs. Collins said in surprise. "You poor things need a good sit down after all you've been through. Your wife's in there, Mr. Kemp. Anna will bring you a cup of good hot tea."

Anna went into the café and there were more people in there than she'd ever seen. If only it could always be like this! Not that she wanted accidents to bring in customers. Far from it. The thought of the wrecked caravan hurt her deeply. Then, just for a moment, as she stood with a tray in her hands, she had a strange feeling inside. It came just as she had been about to accuse God of not caring enough for people. After all, this was the first day of this family's holiday.

Then the strange feeling was gone. Anna tried to recall it. A very strange feeling that everything was under God's control. Everything was in his hands. But the feeling had gone completely now. She shook her head. Who could know God well enough to understand him, anyway?

Slowly Anna went into the bungalow. As she

pushed the door of the living room open, Matthew's parents were leaning forward, probably looking at their phones and wondering why they couldn't get a signal. Then she nearly dropped the tray in surprise. They were both praying! She stood and watched for a moment. Even a gentle cough failed to stop them. Then quite suddenly they looked up at her and smiled.

To Anna's surprise, she felt far more awkward than they did. If anyone had caught her praying like this, she would have been *so* embarrassed!

"Thank you," Matthew's mum said, standing up and taking the tray. "That's so kind of you. When your mother's free, could you ask her to come in. We have to find a place to sleep tonight, and she may know somewhere close. We'd like to leave the caravan here if we can, and we'll arrange to have it taken away as soon as possible."

Anna said, "I'll see," out loud, but inside a fantastic idea had come to her. She'd say nothing about it to the Kemps now, but she'd tell her mother as soon as she was free. "I'm going back to the kitchen to help," she said.

Mrs. Collins was nearly through with serving food and drinks. A couple of other trucks had been attracted into the café through seeing the other vehicles parked outside. The breakdown crew had gone off quickly as they had other work to do. The caravan was dumped in a corner of the yard, but there was no sign of Matthew with Chip.

"They want to know where they can stay, Mum. There's nowhere around I can think of."

Mrs. Collins frowned. "Mrs. Myers down at the farm might help if it's only for a night or two. She sometimes takes in visitors."

Anna tried to sound casual as she emptied one of the jugs of now-cold tea into the large sink. The tea bags fell out with a thud. "It's a shame, really, that we don't do bed-and-breakfast here at the café." She looked up out of the corner of her eye to see her mother's reaction.

"Love you, Anna, where would we ever put people up? The bungalow's only large enough for the two of us, and we could hardly sleep people in the café — unless they slept on the tables!"

"Or under them!" Anna added with a smile, but her heart had sunk deeper than her mother could ever know. It had seemed such a wonderful idea at the time. She knew that if this was her own place she'd do everything possible to help this family for the night. She'd give up her own bed if necessary. But she knew her mother was right. There just wasn't enough room for anyone else to stay, and it would surely be unhygienic to have people sleeping in the café, and probably against some sort of law.

"They want to see you when you're free." Anna pointed into the bungalow, but kept her head turned so her mother wouldn't see the rim of wet around her eyes. "Please, Mum, try and help them all you can. They seem ever such nice people."

Mrs. Collins pulled off her apron and tidied her hair, using a small mirror behind the kitchen door. "I'd best go and see them. They'll be wanting to be off as soon as possible if they have to find a place for the night. You go and ask those drivers if they want anything else to eat."

"Mum," Anna called, "they can have my room if they like. I can sleep on the floor somewhere."

The door closed. Anna knew her mother hadn't heard. Or, if she had heard, she wasn't going to take any notice. And, Anna thought in disgust, if you don't listen, you might as well not be spoken to!

There was a knock from the café counter. The driver with the broken down truck was standing there.

"It doesn't look like I'm going to get the truck fixed tonight after all. Do you know anywhere I can stay? You don't do bed-and-breakfast here by any chance."

"No, we don't!" Anna snapped rudely. "Not by any chance!" With that she tried to push her way past the driver to get out into the yard to look for Matthew and Chip.

The driver caught hold of her arm and held her gently but firmly. Anna tried to fight her way free as all the upset and emotion of the afternoon came out.

"Let me go." she whispered fiercely. "Let me go!"

The other drivers looked up in surprise from their tables. Anna hated making a show of herself. She relaxed immediately. "I'm sorry," she blurted out, and as soon as the driver let go of her arm she ran back into the shelter of the kitchen.

The driver followed. "I feel a bit the same way myself," he admitted. "Only I'm worried about my load. That truck doesn't lock properly. I suppose it will be safe enough in the park here, but you never know."

Anna was facing the other way, drying her eyes on a paper towel. "Do people steal from trucks?" she asked in surprise.

"Steal from trucks? Steal *from* them, *and* steal them. It happens a lot. Perhaps I'll sleep in the cab. I've got a sleeping bag rolled up under the seat. Why, whatever's the matter, girl?"

Anna's eyes, which had been dull and wet a moment before, flashed with excitement. "You'll have see my mum. She won't mind. I've got to go now. I've just had a fantastic idea. Sleeping bags. Of course. Sleeping bags and mattresses. What a great idea!"

Chapter Four

ANNA'S QUESTIONS

The truck driver stared in obvious surprise as Anna rushed from the café. There had been such a sudden change of mood. Her rage had vanished.

"Sleeping bags," she muttered to herself. "There'll be sleeping bags in the caravan. *Matthew!*"

There was no reply from Matthew.

"Chip!" Anna began to call. "Chip, Chip, Chip!" She wandered through the dusty truck park, and made her way through the gap in the fence that led into the small wood. This was quite a likely place for a dog to have got lost. She had a secret hideaway in here. She'd started building it the first day she arrived. At least, she'd marked out some suitable bushes, and come the next morning with some wood and plastic sheeting. After that there hadn't been much time for building hideaways. There had been the café and bungalow to clean and tidy. The previous owners had left it in such a mess! Anna remembered what her mother had said their first evening together.

"If it was always in this state, it's a wonder anyone bothered to stop here."

And that is what nobody did bother to do! Anna smiled a little now. This afternoon had brought in more trade than they'd ever known. She felt sorry for Mr. and Mrs. Kemp with their wrecked caravan, of course.

She sat on the old stool in her hideaway, and hung her head down and rested it in her hands. She felt sorrier still for Matthew. He'd lost his dog.

"Chip!" a voice called suddenly from close by. "Where are you, Chip?"

"Matthew?" Anna called out. "That you, Matthew?"

Matthew pushed his way through into the bushes in surprise. "I didn't know you were out here. Is this your den? Great place."

"It's not a den," Anna said, slightly more sharply then she intended. "It's a sort of private hideaway. I come here when I want to be alone and think."

Matthew just shrugged, seemingly not bothered by the putdown. "I still can't find Chip." He sounded out of breath.

"Well," Anna said quietly, "you can't leave here until you've found him. You'll all have to stay the night."

"Is this a hotel as well?" Matthew asked in surprise, as he sat down on the ground beside Anna.

"It's a transport café," Anna explained. "Truck

drivers don't sleep in hotels. They have bed-and-breakfast."

"Then do you do bed-and-breakfast?" Matthew asked.

Anna shook her head. "No."

Matthew began to laugh. "What do you do then? Bed and no breakfast?"

"No."

"Breakfast and no bed?"

"Oh, Matthew," Anna also laughed, "you're funny. We don't have anyone staying the night. But I suppose you're right, we do serve breakfast to drivers who've been driving all night, so it must be breakfast and no bed."

"Then how can *we* stay the night?" Matthew demanded. "What's your name again? Anna did you say?"

"Yes, Anna. And you're Matthew, aren't you? I haven't asked my mum yet, mind. I just thought you and your parents could sleep in your sleeping bags in our bungalow. None of your bedding got damaged in the accident, did it?"

"Don't think so. Got tossed around a bit, probably, but I didn't see any of our bedding lying in the road with our other things. Sounds a great idea. Let's go and ask my mum and dad. I like it here." Matthew sounded serious for a moment. "We were on our way to the seaside. I was looking forward to that. Anyway, this could be just as much fun. I wouldn't have had anyone for company at the seaside, and I'm fed up with being on my own."

"Same here," Anna admitted. "Nothing exciting has ever happened here as far as I know, but it might. One of the drivers just now said that there are truck thieves about."

"Hijackers," Matthew said. "That's what they call them. They steal a truck from a park like this when the driver's inside having a cup of tea. Then the next day the police find the truck somewhere down a country lane, and it's empty. All its valuable load has been stolen."

Anna stared open mouthed. She wouldn't say so, but fancy Matthew knowing all this about trucks, which was more than she did. And her father had been a truck driver!

"Sometimes," Matthew continued, "the driver is working with the gang and he helps them. He *pretends* the load got stolen when he was in having tea. Here's the café. Let's go in and ask about staying the night. I think it will turn out to be exciting after all."

"Oh, so do I," Anna said in a quiet sort of voice. "Turn out to be very exciting."

Anna, with Matthew following closely behind, ran into the bungalow full of hope. Mrs. Collins was discussing something with Mr. and Mrs. Kemp. She raised a hand to quieten Anna and Matthew as she talked.

"Yes, of course you can leave the caravan here for a few days. I just wish I knew of somewhere close at hand where you could all stay while you're sorting out the insurance and the repairs."

"It's all right, Mum, we know what they can do." Anna ran forward and held her mother's hand.

"Just a minute, Anna, I'm talking."

"But, Mum...."

"Stay outside with Matthew for a bit longer. Go and see if everyone's happy in the café."

"They'll ring the bell on the counter if they need anything," Anna said. "Anyway, this is much more important."

Her mum shook her head. "Not now, Anna. All right?"

But it wasn't all right. Anna spoke up plainly. "Don't send them away, Mum," she pleaded. "Matthew and I have an amazing plan. They can bring their sleeping bags and mattresses in from the caravan and sleep on the floor here."

Mrs. Collins laughed, but gently. "You're a kind girl, love, but these people want a proper bed to sleep in."

"I don't see why," Anna protested. "It would be exactly the same as sleeping in the caravan. Same bedding and everything."

Mrs. Collins began to say, "You two don't understand how grownups...." and then she stopped in surprise. Matthew's parents were looking at each other. Anna could see a smile of understanding and relief on their faces. Her mum seemed to notice it as well.

"Would you...? I mean," she said, "you're very welcome to, of course, but I didn't think...."

Anna smiled at her mum's confusion, and gave her a big hug. "Oh, Mum, you're lovely. I just *felt* we couldn't send them away for the night."

Mrs. Collins began to laugh. She stood up. "That seems to be settled then, if it's all right with you folks. We'll try and make things as comfy for you as we can. But, Anna," she said, holding up a hand again in warning, "you're not to ask anyone else in for the night. That driver with the broken down truck will have to find accommodation for himself down the road."

"That's all right, Mum. He's going to sleep in his cab in the park out there if he can't get his truck fixed in time."

"Oh, is he? And who said so, may I ask? Not....? Oh, Anna, whatever's got into you today?"

"Well, I didn't exactly say he *could*, but then I didn't exactly say he *couldn't*. I sort of felt sorry for him. Besides," she added, with a sudden smile, "if he's around in the morning he'll have to come in and buy a breakfast."

As everyone laughed, Anna felt she wasn't going to be told off for this act of kindness.

"All right, Anna, tell him from me it's okay."

Mr. Kemp said he would pay, of course, for sharing the bungalow, but all Anna's mother said was, "We'll see."

Matthew's parents said they'd go out and inspect the damage to the caravan, and bring in their bedding. Anna and Matthew went with them. The truck driver was in the park, and explained that he definitely had to wait until the morning for the breakdown truck. His hands were filthy.

"Trying to fix it myself," he explained, wiping black oil from his hands with an old rag. "The boss says I've got to try, because he's busy on another breakdown." He walked across to Anna. "What did your ma say about tonight?" he asked quietly.

Anna nodded. "That's all right, I fixed it with her. I'll try and get you a blanket later." She looked at the man's grimy hands. "Yuk! You'll have to wash first though. Mum's ever so particular about keeping things clean."

The driver smiled. "Thanks for the tip. I wouldn't like to get on the wrong side of your ma. She's nice, mind. Don't misunderstand me. Nice, but firm. What did you say your name was? Collins?"

"Yes, I'm Anna Collins."

"Collins, Collins. I'm sure I've met your ma before. Did you have another transport café somewhere?"

"No, we lived in the city. Always lived there.

Mum had to work in a factory canteen after my dad died. That's where she got the idea of opening a place of her own, but we had to wait ages for the insurance to come through. We've only been here four weeks. What we need is plenty of days like today."

The driver frowned in surprise. "What? Accidents?"

Anna gasped in horror. "No, not accidents. I didn't mean accidents. I just meant plenty of people dropping in."

"Perhaps you'll be lucky. Word soon gets round. I've always been told to avoid this place like the plague. I'll see what I can do. I've not known a nicer café, or nicer people, than this. By the way, call me Pete. I'm Pete Morris."

Anna glowed with pride inside. But instead of thanking the man, she felt awkward, and ran off to join Matthew. But she did manage a little wave and a smile. "See you," she called.

"I'm going to keep looking for Chip," Matthew said, after he and Anna had spent more than an hour trying to track him down. It would be dark soon. Matthew seemed rather quiet. He said it was so unlike Chip to run away, but that was the only possible explanation. He and Anna had looked everywhere close to the Old Barn Café.

Silently, he and Anna walked through the woods until they came to the hideaway. They sat down there together to think.

"You know all the places round here," Matthew said. "Is there anywhere a dog could get trapped? Or stuck?"

Anna shook her head. "Do you ever pray?" she asked, all of a sudden, the question seeming to hit Matthew with such force that she might as well have thrown a stone at him.

"Pray?" he repeated, looking embarrassed. "Of course. Everyone does."

Anna was curious. Matthew didn't seem to like the question, but hadn't she seen his parents praying in the bungalow? She'd always been interested in God. Her father used to take her and her mum to church every Sunday. Since his death, Anna had asked so many questions about God and heaven and Jesus, but her mother had no answers. Not real answers. Anna felt disappointment again now. Matthew wouldn't have any answers either. It was the same everywhere. No one had answers about important things like that.

"I was thinking," Anna said, half out loud, and half to herself, "I was thinking, if God listens, you could pray now that we'll find Chip."

"Could do, I suppose. It's worth a try."

"Go on then."

"What do you mean?"

"Go on, pray."

Matthew looked surprised. "What, now? Here?"

"Yes, I'd like to hear how you do it."

Matthew seemed uncomfortable by Anna's matter-of-fact way of putting things.

"Go on, Matthew, I'd like to hear you. No one ever showed me how to pray properly, and it never seems to work for me."

Matthew, though he wouldn't dare admit it to anyone, knew that Anna had a point. It didn't work for her, and it didn't work for him.

Anna sounded puzzled and annoyed. "Oh well, we won't bother then. Perhaps it's more for grownups."

Matthew didn't reply. He'd been going to say that God listens to everyone. Deep down inside, though, he knew he hadn't found that to be true. For the first time in his life he realised he didn't know God in the way his parents did. And it had taken Anna and a lost dog to make him see it. Instead of being grateful, he stood up quickly.

"You go back and see to the café. I'd rather be on my own looking for Chip." Then he sensed Anna was upset by what was happening. "We're still friends," he assured her. "But I want to be on my own. If I'm not back in an hour, send out a search party for me. I might be stuck in a trap with Chip!"

Anna smiled. "I'll cook you a special meal. We'll eat it at a table together. Just the two of us — if you don't get stuck in a trap!"

Matthew pushed his way out of the hideaway

through the overhanging branches. “Okay. That sounds like a good idea to me. And by the way, I still think this is a den.”

Anna stood and watched him go out of sight. Then she shrugged her shoulders and wandered back to the café, deep in thought.

Chapter Five

HIJACKED!

Anna woke early, feeling excited. It was Saturday morning. Saturday was usually no different from any other day – except there might not be any drivers at all stopping at the Old Barn Café.

"Matthew and his parents are taking me for a drive," she said to herself, pulling her pillow up into a ball so she could look out of her bedroom window at the trees in the wood.

Matthew and his parents were cosily settled in the living room of the bungalow. The driver with the broken down truck was sleeping in his cab. It seemed peaceful, and only just getting light. She looked at the clock by the side of her bed. It said half past five. She ought to try and get back to sleep again.

Something must have woken her, for normally she slept until half-past six or even seven. It might be the thought of the trip out. Matthew's parents had promised to take her out in the car. Not to the seaside, which is where she would have specially liked to go. That was much too far.

No, it wasn't the excitement that had woken

her. It was someone walking around in the bungalow. Creeping around would be a better description. Then, as she listened to every sound, she heard the door that led into the café creak as it was opened. Then there was silence. Someone was going out — not coming in. She went to her bedroom window, where she could see across into the café if she leaned out. She drew her curtains back and opened the window wide.

It couldn't be Pete from the broken down truck. Her mother had locked and bolted the outside door for security, as she always did. Pete had been perfectly happy about that, and said he quite understood.

"It must be Matthew," she said to herself. "I wonder what he's up to. I'd better go and check."

She got dressed quickly. Perhaps Matthew was hungry. She could get him some breakfast if he wanted it. Her mum wouldn't mind. But Matthew oughtn't to help himself without asking. That would be wrong, and Anna had a very clear idea of what was right and what was wrong.

The café was empty and so was the kitchen at the back. Then Anna noticed the door into the truck park was unbolted. She let herself out and wandered towards the wood. Perhaps Matthew had made for her hideaway.

And she was right. Matthew was sitting on her old stool, looking thoughtful. "I wish I could find

Chip," he said, looking up as Anna pushed her way in. He showed no surprise at seeing his new friend, and might even have been expecting her.

"I'll help you look," Anna promised. "Do you want some breakfast first?"

"Milk," Matthew said. "I'd like a glass of milk if you can spare any."

"Milk," Anna repeated. "Yes of course. You need something to eat as well, but the sooner we have breakfast, the more time we'll have looking for Chip."

As they made their way back to the café for a quick breakfast, Anna noticed to her surprise that the broken down truck seemed to be deserted. Usually the windows steamed up when people slept in their cabs overnight. On this truck the windows were fully open on each door. Surely the driver wouldn't have slept like that.

"Do you think Pete's in there?" she asked.

"I'm sure he's not. He probably got a lift to somewhere last night."

"Then why did he leave the windows open? It's not going to keep thieves or hijackers out."

Matthew didn't answer. The dusty gravel crunched loudly under their feet.

"I don't usually come out here early like this," Anna said suddenly. "Just listen to those birds. Everything sounds so much louder and clearer. Even the air feels cleaner. Mind you, it was nice in the city. I've only lived out in the country like this for a few weeks. Have you ever lived...?" Anna stopped in annoyance. Matthew didn't seem to be listening to what she was saying.

He took hold of her arm. "Did you hear Chip?"

"What, barking? I didn't hear any barking."

"It wasn't barking," Matthew explained, sounding excited now. "Chip doesn't bark. He just makes noises. But I know it's him all right. Quite close, somewhere."

Matthew seemed convinced that the sound he could hear was coming from the truck park or even the Old Barn Café.

Anna thought she heard something scuffling around in the wood, and went to investigate. She turned round to find that Matthew hadn't followed. To her surprise he was hanging onto the driver's door of the truck and peering into the cab through the open window.

Anna was suddenly not at all convinced that Pete wasn't in there. She made frantic movements with her arms. "Get down! It's rude to stare in like that."

Matthew jumped down to the dusty ground. "Like I said, it's empty."

"Then what were you looking for?"

"Chip."

"What, in the cab? I didn't know he could drive!" Anna began to laugh, but Matthew didn't seem to be amused.

"He's around here somewhere. I heard him. Help me find him, Anna."

Her new friend sounded so serious that she stopped laughing and jumped up to look into the cab. Then she heard a sound that could be a dog whining.

"Chip?" she called softly, unable to see a dog in the cab. The driver's sleeping bag was rolled up on the passenger seat, but otherwise the cab was empty. Where could Pete have gone? And where on earth was Chip?

Anna lowered herself down carefully. Compared to a car, the cab of the truck was so high off the ground! Not only Chip, but now Matthew seemed to have disappeared. She bent down and looked under the truck. Lying on the ground below the brake pipes and transmission was Matthew, tapping on the underneath of the floor and calling quietly to his dog.

As Anna watched in amazement, Matthew crawled out, his clothes dusty and the knuckles on his right hand black with oil and grime where he'd been tapping on the floor.

"He's in there," he announced joyfully, jerking a thumb in the direction of the truck.

"What, in the back of the truck?" Anna found that hard to believe.

Matthew was making his way round to the rear

doors. “I heard him. He never barks out loud. He just makes his own special noise. Put your ear to the side, and you’ll hear him scratching and whining. How do we get in?”

Anna listened. Yes, certainly there was something moving about in there. “Perhaps it’s Pete. He might be sleeping in there instead of the cab.” Then she remembered she’d seen the rolled up sleeping-bag on the seat. “Okay, so it’s probably not Pete.”

Matthew shook his head. “Pete Morris wouldn’t make a noise like Chip — asleep or awake. And why would he be scratching around like that? I’m going to break in.”

“You won’t need to break in,” Anna said, remembering what Pete Morris had told her yesterday. “The back doors won’t lock properly. He said that’s why he was afraid of truck thieves.”

“Never mind the truck thieves,” Matthew said, sounding angry. “That driver is a dog thief. He’s shut Chip in there and he’s hoping we won’t find out. Come on, give me a hand with these doors.”

Anna felt excited and frightened at the same time. The doors were so high up, it would be difficult to reach the large lever that must be the handle. Besides, wouldn’t they be in trouble if they were caught?

“Hurry up,” Matthew urged. “Pete Morris might be back at any moment.”

Anna bit her bottom lip gently and nodded. “Okay.”

“You’re frightened.”

She took this as an accusation rather than concern on Matthew’s part. “No I’m not.”

“Then I’ll lift you up, and you turn the lever.”

Matthew seemed strong as he lifted her up in the air. She could touch the lever, but she wasn’t able to move it. Then, just as Matthew seemed to be running out of puff – success! The lever turned and Anna and Matthew fell back in a heap on the gravel.

As they picked themselves up, the right-hand door swung slowly open. Inside they could see mountains of cardboard boxes.

“I wonder what’s in them,” Anna said, brushing the dust from her jeans.

“Never mind the boxes,” Matthew said impatiently, climbing onboard. “Chip’s in here somewhere. I can hear him.”

Anna climbed up and joined Matthew. He’d pushed his way past the boxes to the front of the truck.

“Here he is,” Anna heard him call. “He’s managed to get himself trapped behind these boxes. Come on, Chip, you poor old dog. What have they done to you, then?”

Anna made her way round to join Matthew. From the yard came the sound of dust and leaves blowing in a sudden gust of wind. The rear door of the truck slammed shut and they were trapped in the darkness.

"Open it," Matthew called. "I can't catch hold of Chip. He's ever so frightened."

Anna was really scared now, but she was determined not to show it. "Hang on, I can't see the way to the doors. Yes, all right, I'm nearly there. No, wait, there's no handle on the inside. You come over."

"Hang on, then. Ow! That box was sharp. Ah, that's better. I can see a bit. My eyes are getting used to the dark. That you? Right, where's the handle?"

"There isn't one," Anna explained. "That's what I was saying. There's a sort of rod thing that goes down into the floor, and up into the roof. See if you can help me move it."

They pulled and then pushed at the mechanism. It seemed to be jammed. They could now see their way around inside the truck quite well through cracks of light coming around the doors.

"Listen," Matthew said suddenly. "There's someone out there."

"Let's call for help. *Mmmmm*. Ow, what did you do that for?"

Matthew, much to Anna's surprise, had put his hand over her mouth. He shook his head and put his fingers to his lips as he released her.

"It might be the driver."

"So?"

"So he hid Chip in here. He's up to something, but I don't know what. Or maybe it's somebody else."

"Truck thieves?" Anna suggested.

"Might be. Something like that, anyway."

The truck swayed a little and the cab door slammed shut.

"Now what?" Anna asked.

"Stay put. He can't go anywhere until the truck's fixed. In a couple of hours everyone will be up and we can shout for help when we hear them in the yard."

A couple of hours? Anna shuddered. That sounded like a very long time.

"Get your phone out," she said suddenly. "We can phone my mum." Then she thought. "No, that won't work. There's no mobile phone signal here."

"I don't have my phone with me," Matthew said.

"Why ever not?"

"Why would I? I was going out to look for Chip. Have you got yours."

"No. Anyway, Chip doesn't have a phone, so there'd be no point in you phoning him." She meant it as a joke, but Matthew still didn't seem to be in the mood for any sort of joke.

Someone was sitting in the cab. And that someone might be dangerous.

What was happening now? The engine was

starting with enough noise to wake everyone up. Then, all of a sudden, the truck jerked forward. Anna fell on top of Matthew.

"I'm really frightened," she said, and she meant it.

Matthew stayed sitting on the floor. "What do you think's happening, Anna?"

"I know what's happening," she said, in a quiet voice. "This truck is being hijacked. We're going out onto the road now."

Matthew stayed silent as they felt the truck turn right, and the wheels began to run much more smoothly. The truck changed up a gear and increased speed.

"You're right," he agreed. "The truck *is* being hijacked. *And so are we!*"

Chapter Six

NO ESCAPE

Anna wished she'd stayed in bed at half-past five! Waking up early had only led them into trouble. She might have guessed something like this would happen.

Judging by the small cracks of light coming through the back doors of the truck, it was getting much lighter outside. She frowned. It was Matthew who was to blame. She wouldn't have got up if she hadn't heard him moving around in the bungalow. And if he'd had the sense to bring his phone, they could make a call for help as soon as they were in an area with a good signal. Then, quite suddenly, she felt at peace. It was the same peace she'd felt for a moment yesterday. God was somehow in control.

"Would you have climbed into the truck if you'd been on your own?" she asked.

"Of course. I couldn't let Chip be taken away."

"Then I'm glad I'm with you. It's better if there are two when something scary happens."

"Are you scared?"

"I was, but not now. Are you still scared?"

Matthew was sitting on a large box, with Chip

resting his head on his master's lap. "Not *really* scared. More sort of excited. Where do you think he's taking us?"

"To a quiet lane somewhere. That's what you said they did."

"Did I?" Matthew asked in surprise. "Who are you talking about?"

"Truck thieves. Hijackers."

Matthew was silent for a long time. Then he said, "I wish you hadn't said that. Let's try to escape."

"We can't get out while we're moving. Besides," Anna reminded him, "the doors won't open from the inside. That's how we got stuck in here in the first place. Do you think they'll be ever so angry with us?"

"Who, my parents?"

"No, dopey, the hijacking gang. There might be lots of them."

"I wish you'd shut up about it." Matthew sounded cross now. Anna knew she was to blame. She kept saying silly things. She didn't mean to, but she did.

"Let's pray." That surely must be something sensible to do.

"Could do. Look, Anna, there's something...." His voice tailed away.

"What?"

"Oh, nothing."

"It must have been something."

"All right, Anna, we'll *both* pray — to ourselves."

"You don't mean we pray to ourselves, you mean we pray to God. Anyway, I want to pray out loud," Anna said firmly.

"Go on then."

"I've told you, I'm not sure how."

"Well, don't expect me to show you."

"You're a funny thing, you are," she said. "Your mother and father both pray, so you ought to be able to do it properly as well."

"What makes you think I can't?"

"Well, let's hear you then."

"I wish you wouldn't keep on at me," Matthew said miserably. "You pray your way, and I'll pray mine."

"But I want us to pray *together*," Anna insisted. "I remember my dad telling me about something in the Bible that Jesus said. Something about when two or three people gather together in his name, he'll be there with them." She frowned. "Only I don't know what it means to gather together in his name. It might mean we have to do something special before we start. Do you know?"

Matthew shook his head. "My dad would know. I leave that sort of thing to him. He preaches at our church sometimes, and does all sorts of things there on Sundays."

"Is he a vicar?"

"No, he works in an office in the week. My mum does things for the church, too." Matthew seemed to be more forthcoming with information now. "I'm going to do something like that when I'm grown up." He smiled. "If we're ever hijacked together when we're grown up, I'm sure I'll know how to gather together and pray properly. But right now I don't, so please don't ask me to. Okay?"

Anna felt disappointed, but tried not to show it. She closed her eyes and whispered to God, asking him to keep them safe. But however hard she prayed, she wasn't sure her prayers were getting through. It seemed like there was a high wall between her and God. And if she asked Matthew why this was, he'd only say he didn't know. She missed her dad at times like this. He would have had all the answers. He'd have known how to gather together.

"The driver doesn't know we're here," Matthew said suddenly. "When we stop and he opens the back doors, we'll jump out and run away as fast as we can."

It sounded like a good idea, and Anna nodded in approval.

"Of course," Matthew added, "there might be lots of them waiting to unload these boxes. We might jump straight into their arms!"

It didn't sound like such a good idea after all. "Perhaps Chip would frighten them away."

Matthew laughed. "Chip couldn't frighten anyone, even if he *wanted* to. He's just a great big softie. Aren't you, Chip!" He bent down and rubbed his dog's head. Anna could hear Chip's tail banging on the floor in pleasure.

"We might as well make ourselves comfortable, Matthew. I'm going to move some of the boxes and lie down. We'll just have to wait until we stop. It's no use shouting for help. The driver would hear us too."

"We could shout when we get to the next town. He'll have to stop for traffic lights or something. People walking past would hear us."

Anna shook her head. "That wouldn't work. The driver would jump back into his cab and drive on quickly until he was out in the country. Then he'd stop and catch us. No, our only hope is to wait quietly until he opens the back and then run for it. Everyone will be so surprised that *one* of us might get away."

"Only one of us?" Matthew sounded worried.

Anna laughed. "That's up to you. *I'm* going to get away, whatever happens."

"We'll both get away." Matthew sounded definite. "I wonder how much longer before we stop somewhere."

Anna was trying to look out through a crack between the back doors. "We seem to be on the main road still. The trouble is, I don't know much about the places around here. I can't see any signposts or anything."

Matthew took a turn at looking out. "It's hopeless," he agreed. "You're right, I expect we'll turn off down a small lane soon."

"Soon?"

"Well, he won't risk driving a stolen truck for too long along the main road. It might have been reported missing by now. The police could be on the look-out."

"Then I hope they hurry up and find us — I'm starving hungry!" Anna patted her middle. "That's the trouble with getting up so early. We didn't even get our glass of milk. What's the time now?"

Matthew said he had no idea.

Anna went to the front of the truck and made herself comfortable among the boxes. Although they were on the main road, the truck bounced and jerked around a lot, and the driver seemed to be in a hurry. Matthew came over and joined her. Chip gave a long sigh and laid his head on Matthew's lap. Whether he understood what was happening or not, he seemed resigned to the situation.

Then all of a sudden they slowed down and came to a stop. Matthew and Anna jumped to their feet and crept to the back of the truck. Anna peeped through the crack in the door.

"We're not down any lane," she announced. "We seem to be in a town. I can see people's feet walking past. I wish I could see up. I might know where we are."

"Let me have a look."

Anna moved aside for Matthew. Just then a clock began to strike. One ... two....

Anna held Matthew by the shoulder. "... Six ... seven...." she finished. "Seven? Is that all?"

Matthew came away from the door. "I suppose we've been going an hour. I think we got hijacked about six."

"How much longer do you think we'll be going, then?"

"Not much.... Listen. The driver's got out. Get ready to run for it when he opens the doors. Chip. Chip, come here, there's a good dog."

They waited. They waited, and they waited. No sign of the driver.

Matthew turned round to look at Anna. "He seems to have left us."

"Why would he do that?" Anna asked.

"Perhaps someone from the gang will take the truck on from here."

"Then let's bang on the walls for help. There seem to be plenty of people about."

"No, don't." Matthew held out a hand to stop her. "The driver might be leaning against the side, waiting for the rest of the gang. The only way to get away is to surprise them. We won't surprise them if they know we're in here."

Anna was studying the rear doors. With the truck standing still, it was easier to see how the locking mechanism worked. Matthew noticed what she was doing and knelt with her.

"Try and pull the doors tight shut," he said. "If we take the load off the mechanism I might be able to move this bar. That's what we've got to do. Move this bar."

Anna pulled the doors inwards so hard that she began to shake.

"Harder, Anna."

"I ccccan't!"

"Hold it there, then. That's it. It's moving."

At that moment there was the sound of the driver's door slamming, and the engine roared noisily into life.

"Quick!" Anna said.

"All right, it's coming. *There!*"

But just as the catch came free and one of the doors swung open, the truck lurched forward.

"Get Chip," Anna said, for the dog had run among the boxes in fright. "We can't jump out without him."

"We can't jump out anyway," Matthew said. "We're going too fast."

The open door of the truck began to swing wildly. Anna and Matthew stepped back in alarm. If the truck jerked now, they would be thrown out onto the road.

"Where are we?" Matthew asked.

"No idea."

There was only open countryside, with a small town disappearing in the distance. The truck took a left hand bend rather fast. The door swung open wider, straining on its hinges. Then it swung back with a great crash. They were trapped in the dark again.

The driver jammed on the brakes, sending Matthew and Anna flying back against the pile of boxes.

"Now what?" Anna asked, rubbing her head.

"The driver's getting out. He's coming round to see what's happened. That's what!"

Chapter Seven

A PHONE CALL

With its engine stopped, the truck was now completely silent. They seemed to be parked on loose gravel, because the driver's feet made a scuffing sound, just like they did at the Old Barn Café.

Both Anna and Matthew turned their heads to follow the sound of footsteps as the driver walked round to the back of the truck. They could hear every move he made. At the back, the driver paused. Then there was a rattle on the lever as though it was being moved.

Then the door opened very slightly.

"Get ready to jump," Matthew whispered.

"I'm ready," Anna said, but so quietly that she thought Matthew hadn't heard.

The door shut again and they could hear the lever being moved. Then there was silence. A car passed by. Then silence again. Anna and Matthew looked anxiously at each other as the footsteps began walking round to the other side of the truck.

"Sssh," Anna warned, as Matthew tried to look out through the small hole Anna had noticed earlier between the doors. "Don't move yet."

Suddenly the driver began whistling, jumped back into his cab, and started the engine. The truck moved off.

"I was ever so scared," Anna said, as she and Matthew settled down on the boxes once more. She no longer had that sense of peace. "Ever so scared."

"Me too."

"I didn't think boys got scared easily."

Matthew laughed. "I don't get scared easily, mind," he explained. "That was scary, though. That was the scariest thing that's ever happened to me in my life."

"And to me. Let's hope it doesn't get scarier than that. Don't forget, we're not out yet!"

<><><>

Anna had slept a little, but Matthew insisted he'd stayed wide awake. Certainly the journey so far had been long, and now they were stopping again. Anna looked at Matthew anxiously.

The truck turned sharply to the right and stopped. Now it was going slowly backwards, the reversing beeper sounding loudly. There were men's voices outside. They must have arrived!

"This is it," Matthew said. "Come here, Chip. We're going to have to run faster than we've ever done before." He turned to Anna, and sounded concerned for her. "You'll be able to keep up, won't you?"

"I expect so. Anyway, don't wait for me. One of us *has* to get away."

"Don't you wait for me either, then."

Anna hesitated. "Well...."

"No, Anna. Don't think of me. Just run for safety as fast as you can and find someone who can help. Ssssh, they're coming round to the back now. Hear them?"

Anna didn't dare answer. The men were talking as they stopped by the rear doors.

"You got here in record time. Are you after a bonus?"

A man laughed. "I just want to get home, but I'll have a bonus if there is one." His voice sounded vaguely familiar. Anna frowned.

"You can go as soon as you've done the paperwork. Got the key?"

"It won't lock. There's something wrong with it. Just turn it.... Hey, what are you kids——?"

Anna and Matthew, their eyes dazzled by the sudden brightness, stared out at two men. They seemed to be in some sort of depot along with several other trucks.

"Come on," Matthew urged, "run for it."

As Matthew jumped down, Chip came with him. Matthew tripped over the dog, and fell headlong into one of the men. Anna landed safely and ran towards the main road. There was a little gatehouse and a long red and white barrier blocking the way.

"Stop her, Ted!" one of the men shouted.

A man in a black uniform and a peaked cap appeared from the gatehouse. Anna was too surprised, and too frightened, to dodge round him. She ran straight into his outstretched arms.

"Ow, you're hurting!" she protested, as she was marched back to Matthew, a strong hand gripping her shoulder. "Let me go!"

The man from the gatehouse didn't let go. "What's the trouble?" he asked.

The driver looked closely at Anna and Matthew. "Don't I know you?"

Neither Anna nor Matthew said anything.

"You're the kids from the café." A look of understanding swept over his face. "You got in there after your dog. You did, didn't you?"

Matthew nodded but stayed silent. That was when Anna recognised the man as Peter Morris.

"What's this all about?" asked the man standing with Pete. He seemed to be in charge.

Pete Morris let out a long sigh. "Oh dear, oh dear, oh dear." He turned to the gatekeeper. "It's okay, Ted, I'll see to this. You can go back now."

The gatekeeper turned to the other man, who shrugged his shoulders.

"Yes, go on, Ted, but I've no idea what's happening."

"It's my fault in a way," Pete Morris explained. "It's easy to see what's happened now."

"Then you'd better explain, because I don't understand one little bit."

"Neither do we," Anna added, surprised by her boldness.

Pete Morris spoke to the man who was clearly his boss, while Anna and Matthew listened.

"You told me to try and get the truck fixed, because you couldn't get help until today. Well, I couldn't find anything wrong, so I gave up. I was about to climb into the cab to sleep, when this dog started pawing at the truck door. He'd got himself lost after the accident with the caravan. I popped him in the back of the truck so he wouldn't escape. I didn't want him in the cab with me, spoiling my sleep."

"Why didn't you hand him over to me straight away?" Matthew demanded.

Pete nodded. "It was after midnight. I didn't want to disturb you all because the place was in darkness and the door was locked. So I made myself comfortable and dropped off to sleep. I was going to hand him over in the morning."

Matthew turned to Anna. "Makes sense, I suppose." He turned to Pete. "But how could you drive off if the truck was broken down?"

Pete smiled. "Suddenly I woke up and knew it had to be the fuel filter. I hadn't bothered to check it properly because it was only replaced last week. Sure enough, it was blocked. I needed to let the boss here know not to send anyone in the morning, so I walked to the phone box because I didn't want to wake everyone up to use the payphone in the café. It seemed a long way down the road, but I had a good flashlight."

"He's right," Anna added. "It *is* a long way, in the opposite direction to where the caravan got smashed."

The boss frowned. "Caravan? What caravan? Dogs and caravans. Am I going mad?"

Pete Morris laughed. "I'll explain all about it later. I didn't know if you wanted me to stay put, so I didn't want to wake everyone by starting the noisy engine and driving to the phone, but on the phone you said I was to come here as soon as possible."

"Yes, I did."

"Well, that's what I've done. Only I was so full of wondering how quickly I could get here that I clean forgot about the dog in the back."

"And *we'd* got up early and heard the dog in the truck, but Pete wasn't there," Matthew explained. "When we got in to rescue him, the door slammed shut in the wind. Then the driver came back."

Pete Morris frowned. "Then why on earth didn't you shout for help and bang on the back of the cab?"

Anna turned red. "We didn't know it was you. We thought you were a truck thief. We thought we were being hijacked. Oh dear, are we in trouble?"

"Phew!" Pete Morris said. "You poor kids. You're not in trouble with us, but you will be with your folks. We'd best phone them immediately."

The boss nodded towards the office block. "Go on," he said, "take them in there. They can use the toilets while you use the phone at the Reception desk."

The offices were deserted as it was Saturday. The toilets came as a welcome break. Anna knew the number for her mum's hone in the bungalow, and the driver found the dialling code for her.

"Mum? Mum, this is Anna. We're ... Yes, Mum ... Sorry, Mum, but ... Oh, don't be cross ... Yes, all right ... No, I don't know where we are ... The driver's here. You want to talk to him? ... Yes, all right." Anna, her eyes wet, handed the phone to Pete Morris. "She's ever so mad," she said, "and she wants to speak to you. She says she's already called the police."

The driver pulled a face. "I never did want to get on the wrong side of your ma," he said quietly. "Oh well, here goes!"

The conversation was long. Gradually Pete Morris relaxed. It seemed he was no longer being told off, but perhaps even being thanked for getting them safely to a phone. Then came long discussions on how to get Anna and Matthew back to the Old Barn Café.

"We're at the truck depot in Stenmouth, Ma.

There won't be any trucks going your way until Monday," Pete explained. "No long distance buses I know of, or trains. I could take them back on Monday if you like. ... Yes, we have insurance and the seat belts are fine. ... They could stay the weekend with me and my missus if they wanted to. ... I don't know. I'll see what they say." Pete Morris lowered the phone slightly. "Would you both like to stay here for a couple of nights?"

Anna looked uncertain. "I'm not sure. Did my mum say we have to?"

Pete shook his head. "No, but she wants to know if you'd like to."

Anna turned to Matthew, concerned about staying with strangers. "What do you think?"

Matthew didn't seem to know what to think.

The driver spoke into the phone. "Tell you what, Ma. Let them come back with me and have some lunch. They can see the house and meet my missus. Then we'll phone you back and see what they think about it then."

Anna looked up at Pete Morris and nodded, slightly half-heartedly. As adventures went, this didn't seem to be an especially good one.

"She says yes," Pete said. "All right, Ma, we'll phone you later when we've all had a chance to think about it."

Pete Morris smiled at Matthew and Anna. He seemed friendly enough, and his boss here at the truck depot seemed okay with what was happening. "Your ma says the boy's parents will drive over for you if you don't want to stay. Anyway, that's up to you. We've come a long way, so I don't think they'd get here and back again today, anyway. You're probably hungry."

"Starving," Matthew said. "Really starving. It must be the afternoon."

"Not quite," Pete said, "but we've been on the road for just over five hours, so you can tell how far we've come."

Anna looked around her. They were in a truck park on an industrial estate close to a small town on the side of a hill. "Is that Stenmouth over there?" she asked. "I've never heard of it before, but I heard you telling my mum on the phone about it. Where exactly are we?"

Pete Morris laughed. "Of course," he said, "I haven't told you yet. Yes, this is Stenmouth, and over in that direction is the sea. You're at the seaside now. Feel more like staying?"

Chapter Eight

MORE QUESTIONS

Pete Morris said he wasn't quite ready to leave yet, as he had some paperwork to fill out. He suggested they took Chip for a run in the field across the road.

"The farmer won't mind," he said. "He's a friend of the owner here. But keep to the edge of the field and come back in fifteen minutes."

A run with Chip was another welcome activity after being in the truck for more than five hours. Certainly Chip, the cause of all the trouble, seemed to enjoy it.

Pete Morris and his wife Kate lived in a small terraced house in a narrow road not far from the beach. Pete drove them there in his old and slightly battered car. It swayed and bounced about nearly as much as the truck had done.

"Call me Aunty Kate," Pete's wife said when they arrived. She was small and thin, with her dark hair swept back. She winked at Anna and Matthew when she heard about their adventures. "A right pair of clowns you two are, I must say!"

Anna laughed. She thought she was going to like it in Stenmouth after all. Food was soon served and she and Matthew filled themselves up.

Anna couldn't help noticing that Pete ate even more than they did. Maybe that's what you had to do if you were a truck driver. "Can we go down to the beach?" she asked, when they'd finished.

Kate Morris went to the front door and showed them the way. "Be back here by five, and don't go climbing into any trucks!"

Matthew and Anna laughed as they raced off down the road with Chip. They followed the directions carefully, and there was the sea! A long road — the Promenade — ran to the left as far as they could see. Crossing carefully, and leaning over the white railings, they looked down onto the sand below.

"There are caves in the rocks that way," Matthew said, pointing in the other direction to the Promenade.

"What's going on over there?" Anna asked. She could see some young people gathered in a large semicircle. "Is it some sort of game?"

"That's a beach service," Matthew said. "It's not really for us. Come on, let's go and check out those caves."

Anna leaned further over the railings. The young people seemed to be singing, but were too far away for her to hear them properly. "Why isn't it for us?"

Matthew shrugged. "It's for people who don't go to church. Come on, the tide will reach the caves soon."

"But *I* don't go to church," Anna protested. "I used to, but I don't go anymore. You go to the caves and I'll.... Oh, bother."

Matthew laughed. "Well, there you are then. It's over. That was their last song. They're starting to pack everything away."

"Oh well, we'll go and see the caves, but can we go past them on the way? I want to see what's on that large board."

"Okay, but let's hurry."

A few of the young people were still left in the group, talking to the grownups who must have been running the service. Anna thought it was a bit odd to have a service on a Saturday, because she'd always thought Sunday was the proper day. Now she was even more interested to discover what had been going on.

A man was pulling strips of words from the large board. Only some of what had been on there was left now. Anna stopped to read.

YOU HAVE BEEN
SAVED THROUGH FAITH
(IN JESUS)
Ephesians 2:8

It didn't really mean much to her and she felt disappointed. She'd expected something better than that.

The man took off the words YOU HAVE BEEN, and she thought perhaps it made a bit more sense now. Whatever "Saved Through Faith" meant, she didn't think she had been. Perhaps Matthew had.

"Have you been saved through faith in Jesus?" she asked rather loudly. One or two of the young people turned to look first at her and then at Matthew.

Matthew nodded and looked embarrassed. "Yes, I go to church, see. That's what it means."

"That's what *what* means?"

Matthew was clearly anxious to get away. "If you go to church, and the things you do are all right, then you're...."

"Saved?" Anna asked.

"Yes, I suppose so."

She wasn't giving up. "You don't sound as though you know at all. Anyway, what's an Ephesian?"

The more Anna questioned him, the more Matthew realised he didn't have the answers. But this last question was all right. Yes, he certainly could answer that one. "Don't you really know? Ephesians is a book of the Bible. Those words that were on the board come from the book of Ephesians, chapter two and verse eight. There were some Christians in a place called Ephesus, so the people there were called Ephesians. Saint Paul wrote a long letter to the church, telling them things like that verse that was up there on the board. It's all been taken down now, but that's where it comes from."

"Fancy you knowing all that," Anna said in admiration. Then, feeling perhaps she shouldn't be showing how little she knew, she pulled Matthew by the arm and ran with him towards the caves. Chip ran by their side most of the way, when he wasn't chasing seagulls.

The rest of the afternoon passed quickly, although they were careful not to be late back at the Morris's house.

"Aunty Kate," Anna said, "you're ever so lucky living here right by the sea."

"Yes, I know I am, but we enjoy it best of all later in the year, when the holidaymakers have gone home. And in the spring, of course. Perhaps best of all in the spring. That's when the air seems at its freshest and purest, and the sand is clean. Now then, I'm sure you'll be wanting tea. Pete will be back soon. He's had to go back to the depot to help. He works for a haulage company."

"Was that an important load?" Matthew asked. "Was it ever so valuable?"

Kate Morris laughed. "Must have been, I suppose, the fuss he was making over it. Part of his load was machine bits or something that were needed for Monday at a factory twenty miles north of here. That was only a part of his load, and they'll be using a small van to take them on to there. Spends most of his time, Pete does, running around the country chasing up bits and pieces."

"Is that what they do at the truck depot?" Matthew asked, who was becoming interested in industry and factories. There were several large industries near where he lived, and he was fascinated to see the men and women going into them on his way to school.

"I don't know, love. You'd best ask Pete when he gets back."

"Could I phone my mum again?" Anna asked suddenly. "We didn't bring our mobile phones with us."

"Why, of course. You're welcome to use my mobile. First, let me phone Pete and tell him to meet us down on the seafront as soon as he's free."

Once Anna had got through, her mum had plenty to say to her. She was no longer cross, but wanted to make sure Anna really did want to stay away for the two nights.

Then Matthew spoke to his own mother. He talked for ages. They agreed to stay until Monday, when Pete would drop them back in his truck. Eventually Kate Morris had to tell Matthew to hurry up.

"Got to go now, Mum," Matthew said, "but we'll speak again tomorrow. 'Bye!"

"Sorry to rush you," Kate said, "but Pete will be looking all over the place for us. Do you like fish and chips? Good. Pete was already on his way back when I spoke to him. We're going to buy four lots of fish and chips and eat them walking along the beach. It's ages since I did anything like this. We'll have a good time together this weekend. I'm ever so glad you're both staying."

She caught hold of their hands and skipped lightly down the road with them towards the sea, as though she was their age and one of their best friends. Matthew, slightly embarrassed at first, soon entered into the fun, and they arrived breathless at the Promenade.

There was no sign of Pete, and Kate used her phone again to contact him.

After a short phone call, she said, "He can't find anywhere to park our car. That's the trouble with the summer. All these yellow lines in the road. He wants cod, and he'll see us by the steps."

Anna suddenly felt awkward. "We don't have any money with us."

"Don't worry, I'll pay," Kate said. "Your parents can sort it out with me later."

The smell from the fish and chip shop drifted across to where they were standing. Although both Matthew and Anna had eaten a good lunch, this would only be their second meal of the day. Anna breathed in deeply. No wonder she felt so hungry!

They had to wait a few minutes for the fish to be freshly cooked, and Pete turned up while they were waiting.

"You were going to meet us by the steps," Anna said.

"I was too hungry to wait," Pete said, laughing. "The gorgeous smell of cooking coming from here must be the best advertisement for food in the whole of Stenmouth."

With their food wrapped in greasy white paper, they made their way to the beach where they opened their packages. The sands were much emptier now. The tide was nearly in, but there was plenty of room to walk. Of the beach service there was no trace. The large sign, the young people, the grownups — all gone. Anna tried to remember what had been written on the sign.

"Did you say your name was Collins?" Pete Morris asked, throwing a piece of fish to Matthew's dog.

"Watch out for bones," Kate warned him. "Dogs can choke over bones."

"Does he like chips?" Anna asked, giggling. "Is that why he's called Chip?"

Anna wasn't going to find out how Chip got his name, because Pete asked his question again.

Anna nodded. "Collins? Yes, I'm Anna Collins."

"And your dad's dead now, isn't he?"

"Pete!" Kate Morris said, looking daggers at her

husband.

"Oh, that's all right," Anna said brightly. "He died ever such a long time ago."

"And did he drive trucks?"

"Yes, that's one of the reasons Mum opened the transport café. The legal case for compensation for my dad's accident went on for years, but it came through at last so she bought the Old Barn Café with the money. She wanted to help other drivers, but not many of them bother to stop — yet." Anna looked up. "Aunty Kate, Pete is going to tell all his friends, and he's going to *make* them come in for meals!"

Pete Morris laughed. "Well, I'm going to have a good try. But about your dad. I think I used to know him. Was he killed in a driving accident?"

"Yes," Anna said, "but I don't know much about it. Mum won't discuss it with me. I think it upsets her too much. Something to do with the brakes not working properly."

Pete had finished his fish and chips. He rolled the paper into a ball and tossed it into a litter basket. "There's more to it than that. Much more."

Anna felt surprised. "Is there? I didn't know." She could understand her mother's grief, and she'd never pressed her for more information.

"There was this long hill down. Right out in the wilds in Wales, and not a house in sight. All of a sudden his brakes failed. He would have known the hill well, and I'm quite sure he knew he could get down by keeping the truck in low gear. That's how they found the truck — in low gear. He made it round the first two bends all right, but he needed all the road because he was cornering fast. A big truck, it was. Then, as he approached the third bend, there was this family walking in the road. Nobody's fault mind. They were well into the side, but your dad needed all the space."

"Did he...?" Anna froze in horror, realising that this might be the reason she'd been told very little.

"Knock them down? Oh no, Anna, he drove straight through the wall, crashed into a large tree, and saved the family. He died at the spot — a hero"

"Pete!" Kate Morris said, sounding angry, "you mustn't tell her all this."

"Oh no, Aunty Kate, I don't mind. Honest I don't." Anna ran over to Kate and held her hand tightly. "I wish someone had told me before. I'm proud of my dad now I know the brave thing he did. Ever so proud."

Kate Morris waved a hand at her husband and Matthew. "You two go off with the dog for a bit. There are times when people like to be quiet. You stay with me, Anna love. Are you sure you're all right?"

Anna said she'd never felt better. This was one of the best days in her life. The adventure in the back of the truck, and then finding out her father was a real hero.

"Aunty Kate," she asked suddenly, "do you have a Bible back at your house? I want to find out exactly what an Ephesian is!"

Chapter Nine

NOT A REWARD

"I've got a Bible back at home somewhere, if I can find it" Kate Morris said. "It's a nice one I was given by our church some years ago. That's when I was in the Junior Church."

"Do you still go?" Anna asked, always fascinated by churches and chapels, but hardly ever able to go herself.

Kate laughed. "I'm too old, love. You had to leave at sixteen, and that was a few years ago."

"Fancy *having* to leave church. I thought anyone was allowed to go to church."

"What a funny thing you are," Kate Morris said kindly. "I only had to leave the Junior Church because I got too old for it. There was nothing to stop me going to the main church services. The Junior Church was a Sunday youth group."

"Do you still go to the proper church?"

There was a long silence. "No, not now. I went mostly to be with my friends. When we started getting boyfriends we drifted away."

Anna frowned. "That's not what Matthew thinks. He says it's easier to do things like that when you get older."

Kate Morris shook her head. "That's not the way it works, love. But why all this interest in the Bible and church?"

Anna explained how she was never taken anymore, but was always trying to find the answers to her questions. "Grownups never seem to have the answers," she complained.

"Oh dear," Kate said, "and I'm another one without answers, I suppose."

"I'm afraid so," Anna said bluntly.

Kate Morris smiled. "I'll tell you what," she said encouragingly, "it's Sunday tomorrow, and we'll all go to church in the evening. I'd like to look up some of my old friends again."

"I thought they all left the church."

"Well, some did, and some didn't. Some of them had boyfriends from the church and they're probably still going. Yes, we'll all go tomorrow evening. Pete as well, of course — and Matthew."

<><><>

Anna felt so excited, and Sunday morning and afternoon couldn't move quickly enough for her. Matthew didn't seem quite so pleased, and said his church at home was sure to be better than one at Stenmouth.

Evening came at last. It was a nice bright church inside. Everyone sang loudly, although Anna knew neither the tunes nor the words of what sounded like modern worship songs, put up on a large screen. At the front a small band played the music on guitars and drums and brass, accompanied by a keyboard. Matthew seemed to know what they were singing, and he sang as loudly as anyone. Anna enjoyed herself, and couldn't understand why more people didn't go if church services were like this.

As she listened carefully, things began to make sense. Things she'd heard about Jesus and God's love when she'd been to church with her father. But she'd never heard things explained like this before.

Kate had been talking with some people she knew, and then she came across to Anna. "Come on, love, time to go."

Anna looked up. "Sorry, Aunty Kate, I was just sitting and thinking. I can't imagine why you don't come here *every* Sunday."

Kate Morris smiled. "Neither can I ... now. Anna love, I'd like to get you something – as a sort of present. Tell me if you've got one already."

They were near a table covered in books. Kate Morris picked up a fat paperback.

"What is it?" Anna asked.

"It's a Bible."

"In paperback?" Anna asked in astonishment.

"A lot of modern translations are in paperback," a man said, who was standing by the bookstall. "It helps keep the cost down. Have a look through it."

Anna turned some of the pages slowly. “Aunty Kate, where are the Ephesians?” she asked in a loud whisper.

Kate Morris looked awkward. “Towards the back somewhere, I think.”

The man was standing by their side. “Look it up in the index,” he said. “That’s the best way to learn where all the books are in the Bible. It’s nothing to be ashamed of.”

So together Kate Morris and Anna looked up Ephesians chapter two and verse eight.

“It tells us what a *real* Christian is,” Anna said slowly. “It says....”

“Come on,” Pete said firmly. “Kate, you buy it for the girl if you like. There’ll be plenty of time to read that when we get back.”

“Would you like it, then?”

“Oh, yes please, Aunty Kate. If it’s not too expensive.”

It wasn’t. The paperback Bible was bought, and Anna carried it back proudly to the Morris’s house.

As soon as they got in, Pete turned the television on. Anna felt annoyed by this. She’d wanted to read in peace and quiet. There was a film starting that looked quite exciting, but the new Bible fascinated her more.

“Bedtime soon,” Kate Morris warned. “You’re having a room each.”

“I think I’ll go up and read for a bit,” Anna said,

getting up from her chair.

Kate nodded towards Anna's new Bible. "Are you going to have a look at that?"

Anna hesitated a moment. "It's not too late tonight to be reading, is it?"

Pete glanced round from watching the film and smiled. "You read for as long as you like, but don't forget we're making an early start in the morning. We have to collect the truck from the depot soon after seven. Try and be up by six."

Anna felt a little thud of excitement at this. It would be good to be home again. It was nice here in Stenmouth, of course, but it would be nicer still back with her mum. And all the things she would have to tell her!

Anna lay on her stomach on the bed in the small bedroom and turned through the pages of her new Bible. She started reading verses here and there. There were some bits she couldn't understand, but even so, she could see now why her father had enjoyed reading his Bible when he was alive.

Anna paused with the pages open at John's Gospel and turned onto her back and stared up at the ceiling. Fancy her father dying a hero like that. He'd died to save a family walking up the hill.

She frowned. Perhaps it was a bit like that with Jesus. Hadn't the speaker at the church this evening said Jesus died to save people? No it wasn't really the same. Her father hadn't known those people. Didn't Jesus know and love everyone? She turned back onto her front and looked down at her Bible again. John's Gospel. They'd sung something at the church that evening. "Verse sixteen, John's Gospel chapter...." It had rhymed with something. What was it? Calvary. Yes, chapter three. Verse sixteen, John's Gospel chapter three. For the life of her she couldn't remember what the verse was about.

There was a tap at the door. It opened slowly. Kate Morris looked round. "Mind if I come in?"

Anna did mind really, but instead of saying anything, she just smiled. No, perhaps she didn't mind after all. "It's a nice Bible," she said. "Thanks for getting it for me."

"Reading anything special?"

"The Gospel of John. What's a Gospel?"

"Good News. That's what Gospel means."

"Oh. Perhaps there's good news in chapter three. I was just finding verse sixteen. Come and sit on the bed and we'll find it together." Anna experienced a cosy feeling as Kate Morris sat beside her. Although Kate was grown up, Anna could understand her in a way.

Anna read the verse out loud. "'Yes, God loved the world so much that he gave his only Son, so that everyone who believes in him would not be lost but have eternal life.'" She sighed. "I've done all sorts of wrong things. *And* I've said wrong things and thought wrong things. Did God's Son, Jesus, really die instead of God punishing *us*? It sounds too good to be true."

"When you say 'us', are you thinking it was instead of *you*, and instead of *me*?" Kate asked quietly.

Anna nodded. "It must mean me and you when it says *everyone*."

Kate said, "I've never thought of it like that before."

Anna looked up and smiled. "It's either true or it's not true. It can't be a *bit* true. This is either all nonsense, or it's God's word to us. If it's true, oughtn't we to be doing something about it?"

"Anna, love, I've never known anyone ask such searching questions before."

"But it *is* true, isn't it?"

"Oh yes, I'm sure it is. I believe it now like I've never believed it before. What was that verse you were talking about earlier? Ephesians something, wasn't it?"

"Chapter two, verse eight. Funny how I remember that. It doesn't rhyme with anything like this one. You find it. You'll be quicker than me. It's what was on the notice board on the beach yesterday. "

Kate Morris didn't need to use the index this time. "I'll read it out."

Anna wasn't content just to listen. She followed

the words on the page as Kate read. "'For by grace you have been saved through faith. And this is not your own doing; it is the gift of God.' And look at the next verse. 'Not as a result of works, so that no one may boast.'"

Anna frowned. "What are works, Aunty Kate?"

"Some people think they have to lead ever such a good life before God is able to love them. The Bible calls them 'works,' because it's like people trying to work their way to heaven. But good works don't get us to heaven, because there's like a wall between us and God."

Anna gave a long sigh. "I know all about that wall," she said. "I don't think God can hear me through it when I pray."

Kate Morris put her arm around Anna's shoulder. "So much is coming back to me now," she said. "There are lots of places in the New Testament that tell us that God loves us so much that Jesus died on the cross and then risen from the dead. It was instead of *us* being punished for our sins. I once heard a preacher say that it's like a door in the wall that *we* have to open, and no one ever gets turned away. Could you trust God to let what Jesus did on the cross count for you?"

Anna knew about punishment, but she'd never thought of anyone taking a punishment someone else deserved. "I think I could trust *Jesus*," she said slowly.

"Then ask him to help you. That verse says that even trusting is a gift from God. We can ask for that gift. Shall we do it now?"

"We?" Anna asked in surprise. "You won't need to. You're a grownup."

"That doesn't make any difference, Anna. I've never understood it properly before you came here, but you've helped me see that this trusting is for everyone, young *or* old."

"But you know all about it. I think I need to have all my sins taken away, but you wouldn't know all about this if you weren't a proper Christian."

Kate Morris pointed to her head. "I know a lot of it up here, but not down here." She tapped her heart. "I've never asked Jesus to save me and forgive my sins. I thought it would work out all right as I got older. Well, it didn't."

"That's what Matthew thinks. He says...."

"Never mind about Matthew, love. Let's think about ourselves for now. I don't know about you, but I'm going to thank God for loving me, and ask Jesus to come into my life and forgive my sins."

"Pleased do it for me as well," Anna said.

"I can't. Nobody can do it for you. You've got to ask him yourself."

"I didn't know that. I think I'll ask first." She bowed her head. "Thank you, God, for loving me. I've done some very wrong things. But the Bible tells me Jesus died for all of them. Jesus died instead of me being punished for them. Jesus, please make me your own. I'm opening the door to you. Please come in. I don't know much about you yet, so you'll have to teach me ever such a lot. Amen."

Kate Morris prayed, but Anna wasn't listening. She knew that God had heard her prayer. The door in the high wall between her and God was wide open.

Kate Morris looked up, excitement showing in her eyes. "It's just like you said, Anna love. It's either nonsense or it's true. And if it's true, we've got to do something about it. Well, it's true all right. The number of times I put it off. Why ever didn't I do it when I was your age? I knew so much about the Bible and about being a Christian, but I never prayed for it to happen to me."

Anna put her arm round Kate. "That's the first time I've ever heard about it like this. Just think, God loves both of us."

"And he loves Pete."

"Oh yes," Anna agreed, "and Matthew as well. But I don't think Matthew has ever done what we've just done. He seems to think he'll be all right if he leads a good life."

Kate Morris pointed to verse nine. "Don't forget it says, 'Not as a result of works, so that no one may boast."

"Then I'll tell him about it," Anna said.

Kate Morris looked at Anna and saw the fire and excitement in her eyes. She smiled. "I'm sure you will. You'll tell Matthew, and probably lots of other people as well!"

Chapter Ten

THE LONG ROAD HOME

Matthew was feeling really sleepy the next morning when Kate Morris came knocking on his door. He knew they'd be leaving early, but it felt like the middle of the night.

"Six o'clock, and time to get up!"

"All right." He tried to sound awake, but didn't make a very good job of it. In any case, six o'clock was not all right, not after getting up at the crack of dawn yesterday to look for Chip.

He listened. There was Anna out on the landing, humming some song they'd sung at church the night before. Something was happening to Anna that puzzled him. Happening, or perhaps it had already happened.

He yawned loudly and tipped himself out onto the floor. There was a small blue rug for his feet, but he missed it. Then, as he began to pull on his clothes, he started to wake up. He was glad to be going back to his parents, but he'd enjoyed these two days of unexpected adventure.

There was a knock on the door again. "Are you getting up?" It was Kate Morris, apparently anxious to prevent him going back to sleep.

Matthew was pulling on his shoes. “Ready,” he called.

“Good. Breakfast will be in about twenty minutes. You’ve just got time to take that dog of yours for a run on the sands. Pete will be ready to take you both to pick up the truck at ten to seven.”

“Okay. There, I’m coming.” Matthew opened the bedroom door.

Kate Morris gave him a big smile. “Well done. The bathroom’s free, but don’t be late back from the beach.”

Anna called from her room. “I’m just doing my hair. Can I go as well, or do you want a hand with the breakfast?”

“No, you both go and have a run. Stretch your legs as much as you can. You’ll be sitting in that truck of Pete’s for a long time today.”

Matthew enjoyed his time on the beach with Chip. It was properly light now, but there was a soft greyness to the sea. In three or four hours the sands would be packed. Anna had come with him, but she was strangely quiet, and preferred to walk a little way behind by herself.

Back at the house they both ate a good breakfast. Pete got them into his old car at ten to seven, and took them straight to the haulage depot.

The truck they would be using was enormous. Matthew had imagined it would be the one they’d arrived in. Pete walked round the truck, checking the wheels, with Matthew thinking how tough he looked.

Pete turned to Matthew and Anna standing in the depot yard. “There'll be plenty of room for the three of us. I've brought an old rug from the house for the dog and we'll soon have you onboard.”

Pete spread out the rug. Matthew tried to push Chip in, but he refused to go. So Matthew climbed up, dragging Chip in after him. But Chip had other ideas, his claws scrabbling for grip on the side of the cab. Anna gave him a push from behind and he had to follow his master. Matthew thought he looked far from happy.

“Sit down, boy, we'll be going soon.” He gave Chip a pat on the head, and Chip looked up at him with wide staring eyes before lying down on the rug on the floor.

“Do we *have* to?” he seemed to be asking.

Pete jumped in and slammed his door shut. Matthew grinned at Anna and settled down in his seat. They were three in a line. It was going to be a lot more comfortable than it had been sitting on the boxes.

“Seat belts on,” Pete said, as he leaned forward and pressed the starter.

Matthew was surprised to discover how quiet the truck was from inside the cab. As they made their way through the outskirts of Stenmouth, their going was slow in spite of the early hour, and the truck seemed to be forever changing gear. As soon as they left the town, the automatic transmission changed up into a high gear and they were properly on their way.

Matthew leaned forward and looked sideways for a last glimpse of the sea. That would probably be all for this summer holiday. It was unlikely his father would be able to borrow a caravan at such short notice. Anyway, it would be fun at the Old Barn Café with Anna, if they were able to stay on there.

He was thinking how different the view of the road was from so high up. He could see over walls and hedges in a way he'd never been able to in a car. There was no long bonnet in front like the car had, and the road seemed to rush underneath them at high speed. Anna was chattering on, telling him and Pete how she'd asked Jesus to forgive her sins, and take her as his own. Matthew smiled a slightly awkward smile, but was glad for her. As she hadn't been to church much, that was probably just what she needed. He knew there were people, young and old, who needed to do this. Not that he needed to, of course, but it made him feel a little uncomfortable. Surely he didn't need to....

I think I've heard enough of this, he thought to himself, turning to Pete. "Are we going to stop anywhere on the way back?" he asked.

Pete said, "That's just what Kate was trying to tell me last night; what Anna here has just been saying about God. I wonder if I could do it as well." Then he answered Matthew. "Not ready to stop yet, are you! We'll have a break in a couple of hours. There are all sorts of limits on the time we're allowed to drive without a break. *And* limits on how long we can drive on each day. There's a tachograph in the cab that records how long we've been driving without a break, and how fast we've been going. The police sometimes stop us for spot checks. Or if we have an accident or fall asleep at the wheel they'll find out if we've been driving for too long."

Matthew thought it sounded an exciting and tough job. He fancied the idea of getting out and seeing a new part of the country every day.

He'd always thought of trucks as slow. When he was in his parents' car, they were always being held up by them. But in spite of this one being fully loaded, it was only up the steep hills like the one they were climbing now that they slowed at all. The automatic transmission kept changing down through the gears. Pete kept as close to the side of the road as he could, letting the cars past that had collected behind.

"Is that the right time?" Matthew asked, noticing a clock among the row of instruments.

"Ten o'clock," Pete said. "That's right. We've been on the road for nearly three hours now. Time for a break soon. There's a small transport café about five miles on from here." He called across to Anna who was sitting very still and quiet. "Are you feeling okay?"

Anna smiled. "Yes thanks," she replied brightly.

"That's all right then. You don't get travel sick or anything do you?"

Anna shook her head. "I'm only quiet because I'm thinking. I've got a lot to think about."

"This café will give you something to think about, too," Pete said. "It's only small but it will be packed with drivers. You might be able to pick up a few tips to pass on back to your ma. Not that she needs them," he continued hurriedly. "The only problem there is the bad name. As soon as more drivers learn how good it is now, it will be just as full. Tell you what, I'll pass the word around amongst the boys in there."

"Boys?" Anna asked.

"Other drivers. Boys *and* girls sometimes. I'll tell them to make sure they stop. Some of them will be going past there today."

"You can't do that!" Anna said in alarm. "I don't want you to stop people going here. Mum says we've got to look for *new* trade."

Pete laughed. "It's a couple of hours or more to your place. Some of them will be ready to stop again by the time they get there."

"I know it's going to be a long journey,"

Matthew said. "Why didn't you stop anywhere for a break on your way? We'd have been able to escape if you had."

Pete laughed. "Sorry about that. I was in too much of a hurry. I had some sandwiches from the day before and I ate them on the move. The only time I stopped was to buy some chocolate from a corner shop about seven o'clock."

"What about your tachometer and having to stop every so often?"

"I ran it close, but just about managed to keep within the law."

The transport café was no more than a tin hut, with its windows streaming on the inside with condensation. The park was packed with trucks, and the tables inside all seemed to be full.

The men looked up as the three of them entered, and a man called something to Pete. He waved and several men began to joke with him. He was obviously well known and popular.

Pete explained that *no*, Anna and Matthew were *not* his children! Then to Anna's great delight he began to tell everyone about the Old Barn Café.

One driver came across to Anna. "Are you open today?"

"Oh yes," Anna said enthusiastically. "Open until the evening. Do you want to stop there for something to eat?"

"I'm waiting for my mates. We're all on our way

to collect a delivery of new trucks. They'll be picking me up here in a minibus in an hour or so. Do you think you could cope with ten?"

"Ten?" Anna asked, trying not to show surprise. "Of course we could. We could manage any number you like. It's the best place there is around there. You know where it is, don't you?"

"Oh yes, we know where it is all right. Most of us have been poisoned there at one time or another!"

"You won't be poisoned now," Anna said, feeling herself go hot all over. "My mum won't poison you!"

The drivers who were gathered around began to laugh. "I'm sure she won't. That's why we're prepared to give it a try. Ten of us, mind. Don't forget."

Anna wanted to get out now. This might be a good way of getting business for her mum, but the embarrassment of all these drivers leaning over her table was almost more than she could bear.

Then, to her relief, they went back to their own tables.

"What do you want to drink?" Pete asked.

"Coke," Matthew said.

"And me, please," added Anna. "A sticky bun as well. Mum will give you the money when we get back."

Pete waved a hand as though to dismiss the

idea. "We'll see," he said. "One sticky bun coming up."

As some drivers left, more arrived, but Anna, Matthew and Pete had a table to themselves.

Anna's sticky bun was enormous. Her mother had never bought buns as large as this. Perhaps she could get some, if this was the sort of thing truck drivers ate. There was no knife to cut it with, although she could probably have fetched one from the serving hatch. But she felt she'd drawn enough attention to herself, so she nibbled away at it, starting to work around the edges before coming to the cherry in the middle.

Then an unfortunate thing happened. She was busily licking icing from her fingers when she knocked the remains of the bun with her elbow. It fell to the floor with a gentle thud. She held her breath, not daring to look up. No one seemed to have noticed. All the men carried on eating. Slowly she relaxed. She certainly had no intention of eating any more of it. The floor looked decidedly unhygienic.

"Excuse me, miss." A driver on the next table was leaning across. "That your bun down there?"

"What? Bun? Where? Oh no, that's not mine. I finished mine." For some reason the drivers around her seemed to be watching and listening. Anna smiled a forced smile. "I wonder how that got there?"

The man behind the serving counter came across with a brush and swept the embarrassing half-eaten bun up. "Sorry," he said. "Would you like another?"

"It wasn't mine," Anna explained. "I finished mine." She had a definite feeling that no one believed her, and now she'd missed the chance of a replacement. Why couldn't she have told the truth?

As soon as he'd finished, Pete said he was anxious to be off. The driver waiting for the minibus called to Anna as they were leaving.

"Ten of us, mind. Don't forget now."

"We'll be waiting specially for you," Anna said, surprised by how loudly she could call above the general background noise. "We often have dozens of people in at the same time." As she said this, the place turned suddenly silent. Whether it was because she'd been shouting, or because of what she'd just said, she had no idea. The drivers all stared at her, and Pete and Matthew looked surprised.

"Well," she said, when they were outside, "that may have been a bit of an exaggeration."

"It was an out and out lie," Matthew said.

Anna gasped. Matthew was right. And she'd thought she would never tell another lie in her whole life. Now she'd told two straight off. She was as bad as she'd ever been. Did that mean nothing had really happened last night? Had God not heard her after all? Had the door in the wall been slammed shut? Feeling fed up, she climbed slowly into the cab of Pete's truck.

Chapter Eleven

A MEAL FOR TEN

The weather seemed to be turning hotter the further they drove inland. Pete Morris said he'd like to turn the air-conditioning on, but it wasn't working properly. It blew cold air on their feet all the time, instead of up on the windscreen. Matthew agreed it was getting too hot in the cab, but he was worried about Chip getting a chill.

"Put the rug over him, instead of under," Pete said, waving a car past. "Always in a rush, some people. Still, I'd be the same if I had a car that could go faster than mine does. Slower than this truck, that old car of mine is. When I'm out in it, I have to wave the trucks past! Yes, that's it, cover him over well. But make sure his nose pokes out, or he'll not be able to breathe."

Matthew and Anna laughed. They enjoyed being out like this with Pete Morris. Soon Anna was feeling quite sleepy when suddenly she realised she was in familiar countryside. Their long journey was over. Pete turned the enormous truck off the main road and drew into the parking lot of the Old Barn Café. Theirs was the only truck in sight!

Memories came flooding back to Matthew. The family caravan still lay against the hedge at the back of the parking area, the panels ripped and the roof muddy and scratched. That was to have been their holiday home for two weeks at the seaside.

Anna too remembered things she'd nearly forgotten. The sign that needed repainting, the blue curtains at her bedroom window, her mother's washing hanging on the line in the small back yard. And the deserted truck park. Oh yes, that was just the same as ever.

A sign on the door said CLOSED. Anna frowned. The whole place seemed deserted.

"There's a note," Matthew called out. He unpinned an envelope from the bungalow door. "It's for you."

Anna had been feeling anxious. She took the letter with relief. "It says they've — it's from my mum — it says they've gone to town to get some frozen food supplies in your parents' car. We're to wait for them to get back." Anna's face fell. She turned to Pete. "Sorry, you'll not be able to have a meal."

"That's all right," Pete said understandingly. "I'll call in tomorrow on the way back."

Anna was finishing reading the note. She caught hold of Pete's arm as he began walking back to his truck. "Don't go. Mum says she closed up this morning because that's usually the quietest time.

Most times are pretty quiet, I think. She hopes to be back in time for lunch — in case anyone stops! Anyway, there's food for us keeping warm in the oven. For you as well, Mum says."

"Let's go in then," Matthew said impatiently, rubbing his stomach.

Pete seemed glad to be getting something to eat after all. Everything was laid ready for them, and Anna served it up. Pete said he wouldn't be able to stay long, and was soon on his way again. Anna and Matthew watched him drive off, feeling privileged to have travelled so far in that articulated truck.

"That's it then," Matthew said. "Your mum and my parents will be back soon. We'll just explore around while we're waiting. Make sure Chip doesn't run away again."

"He's.... Where *is* he, anyway?" Anna held her hand to her mouth in horror. "He's gone," she gasped. "Gone with Pete. I left him in the truck."

"You did what?"

"It was your fault just as much as mine. Anyway, he's your dog, so you should have woken him."

"Yes, my fault too," Matthew said quietly. "We've done it now, that's for sure. Whatever will Pete do with him?"

"Don't worry," Anna said. "Pete will know what to do. He'll phone us here when he discovers Chip. Anyway, it will be a bit more of an adventure for him."

"It's not funny," Matthew said. "Pete won't be back here until tomorrow. Poor old Chip could *starve* to death in the meantime."

"Stop worrying," Anna said. "Pete will buy him a tin of dog food. Dogs are probably good company for drivers. They can talk to them. Not that they get many answers!"

"I wish you'd stop making fun," Matthew said miserably. "All you can do is make fun."

"He'll be all right," Anna said confidently. "Pete's ever so sensible. I can just see his face when Chip jumps up suddenly at some traffic lights. And talking about food, let's hope no hungry truck drivers call in while we're waiting for my mum. That's just the sort of thing that would happen when Mum's out. By the way, we mustn't forget that those...." She felt the colour draining from her face.

"What?" Matthew asked in alarm.

"Those men. The ten of them. They'll be along soon in their minibus. That's awful. If Mum doesn't get back, we'll just have to apologise and turn them away."

"Those ones from the last café place? If your mum's not back, we'll have to do something," Matthew said. "We *can't* turn them away, after all the promises you made. They could be the ten most important drivers ever for this place. Think of all their friends they'll tell if they have good food. And think what they'll say to their friends if you tell them to go away."

"I know," Anna said miserably. She would have liked to have prayed about it. Earlier that day she would have done, but now she seemed to be making such a mess of things. Perhaps God wouldn't hear her anymore. No, surely once she'd been given this new life in Jesus, he would never take it away. Perhaps all she had to do was to say sorry. That's what she'd do, and then ask God to help her with this minibus full of drivers who were about to descend on them with enormous appetites. So she prayed, and very quickly too. That lot could be arriving any minute!

"Come on, Matthew, let's get everything switched on in the kitchen. They'll be sure to want chips and things. You can make sure the urn's full of water, and we'll get that up to the boil."

Matthew hesitated. "Are you sure it's all right for us to mess about in the kitchen? Your mum won't be ever so cross or anything?"

"My mum never gets very cross," Anna said laughing. "Well, not very often, anyway. I'm allowed to *work* in the kitchen. It's not called *messing about*! Mum's taught me how to do everything safely. Besides, she should be back with your parents at any moment, and then she'll take over. We'll just get things ready. Those men won't want to be kept hanging about."

Matthew smiled. "You always make everything sounds so simple and easy. I'd have given up before we'd even started."

But now he was able to carry out Anna's orders, fairly confident that everything would work out all right in the end. If only he could see things as Anna now did. Did he really need to *become* a Christian? Was it possible just to ask, exactly as you were? Didn't you have to start living a good life and put yourself right with God first?

"When the water in the urn's up to the mark, switch it on to 'Full'," Anna called.

Matthew obeyed, then went to see what she was doing. She explained that she'd switched on the chip fryer, to get the oil back up to temperature.

"We just drop a load of frozen chips into the wire basket and wait seven minutes on the timer," she explained. "Then we can put sausages and things in the other basket. This is the grill. Burgers and things go on there. We'd better switch that on, too."

"Where's all the food?"

"In the freezer."

"Shouldn't we get it out ready?"

"We don't know what they're having yet. Everything we've got doesn't need to thaw out first. By keeping everything in the freezer, it's sure to be always fresh. The only vegetables we have are peas and beans. We heat the beans in the microwave and the peas go straight into boiling water for exactly five minutes."

This kitchen looked strange to Matthew. He was used to an ordinary home kitchen with a small cooker and saucepans. This stainless steel equipment was beyond him, and he was glad Anna seemed to know all about it.

"Here they come!" Anna called suddenly, looking out of the window.

"My parents?"

"No, those men in the minibus. Oh no, I wish they hadn't come so soon!" She felt herself going faint.

"I'll open the door to them," Matthew said, "and try to make them feel welcome."

Anna was alone in the kitchen. No, not alone. She was now a true child of God. Wasn't Jesus with her? If Jesus had managed to feed five thousand people when there was almost no food to go round, surely he could help her now. She had plenty of food, and there were only ten men to feed! What she needed was the confidence to do it properly. So once again she prayed, and felt sure that her prayers had been heard. It was, she realised, just like talking to a friend.

The men were already sitting in the café, talking loudly and joking with each other. Anna put on her mother's apron and walked boldly in with some menus in her hand. She was going to explain that her mother was out but would be back soon, when she thought better of it. These men might get up and go if they thought *she* was going to do the cooking!

The men ordered their meals. There was nothing on the menu that was difficult to prepare. Anna could see how wisely her mother had selected the items.

"And bread and butter," one of the men called out. "For all of us. Plenty, mind. We're hungry."

Anna walked unsteadily back to the kitchen and opened the larder. She beckoned frantically to Matthew to join her. "I don't know where the bread is," she said. "It should be in here. Perhaps we haven't got any."

"We have," Matthew said. "There are two large loaves of thick sliced on the worktop over there."

Anna sighed with relief. "Right then. Make the tea and then butter up both loaves."

"Both of them?"

"Yes, both. They said they were hungry. When they try our cooking, they might only eat the bread!"

Anna read down the list of orders. Then she went to the freezer and opened the packets and selected what had been ordered. It all seemed so easy. The main problem would be getting everything ready at the same time.

As soon as everything was sizzling, splattering

and bubbling away in the kitchen, Anna went in with the mugs of tea Matthew had made, leaving Matthew to keep an eye on things. She felt very grown up in her mum's apron. "I'll get the bread and butter."

"Nice place this. I hope the food's good."

Anna looked at the man who had spoken. "Oh dear," she said, "I hope it is, too!"

The men all looked surprised and Anna could have kicked herself for saying anything. She laughed, but it was a feeble laugh. "I'd better be going back to the kitchen now."

There was a hatch where the drivers usually came to fetch their own meals when they were ready, but Anna kept it closed. She decided that these men were to be treated to table service. It was most important to impress them. An even better reason to keep them seated was that if they came to the serving hatch for their food they could see through into the kitchen, and discover exactly who was doing the cooking.

Before she knew it, she and Matthew had served the meals without any major problems. There was only one slight confusion where a man had been given three sausages instead of two. Anna told him that the extra one would be "on the house," but the man said he was hungry anyway, so wouldn't mind paying for it. Anna and Matthew sat with the men, and told them how they'd thought Pete's truck was being hijacked. The men laughed at that.

"It wasn't funny at the time," Matthew said. "The first.... Hang on, there's a car. I think it's my parents. I'll just go out and see."

Anna was on her feet first. "You stay there, Matthew. There's something I've got to see about."

"But——"

"Sit down!" Anna ordered, smiling but sounding firm. Probably sounding a bit like her mum, she thought

Matthew looked at the men and shrugged his shoulders. "Women!" he said with a sigh.

Anna heard and turned. She pointed at Matthew. "Men!" she said as she raced from the café. She heard the drivers laughing, so they'd probably heard her.

Her mother was just getting out of the car. "Mum, oh Mum, it's good to be back!"

Mrs. Collins embraced her daughter. "Safe and sound? Where's Matthew?"

"He's in the café with the men."

"Men? What men?"

"The men from the minibus. Oh!" Then Anna explained about the promise they'd made to the men earlier in the day. "But they don't know that *we* cooked it. They think *you* did."

"Then I'd better go and put them right!"

"Oh no, Mum, they're enjoying it. Don't go and say anything to put them off."

"I——"

"Oh, come on, Mum. Take your coat off and come in through the back way."

"All right, but if there are any complaints then you'll have a lot of explaining to do!"

"This is my mum," Anna said to the men as they went in. "She owns this place."

"Congratulations, Mrs. Collins," one of the men called out.

"What, on my daughter?"

"No, on your cooking! Best place on this road, that's for sure."

Mrs. Collins looked lost for words, but Anna's face glowed with pride. It might be slow going, giving the old place a good name, but surely word would soon get round.

Mathew had disappeared. Anna found him in her hideaway looking glum.

"What's up?"

Matthew shook his head. "It's Chip. I've got a horrible feeling I'll never see him again."

<><><>

Later that day Anna was talking to Matthew's father. There was something about him that made him easy to talk to. Anna was aware of just how well he knew Jesus. It wasn't long before she'd told him about her new Bible, and how she'd realised she needed that new life in Jesus for herself.

"But it hasn't made me all that good," she

admitted. "I never thought I'd do anything wrong again. But ... but, anyway, I've told God I'm sorry. Is that all right?"

"I'd like to see your Bible," Matthew's father said, without answering the question directly. "I'll show you a very special verse."

"I know about Ephesians two, verse eight."

"A very good verse. Right, here's another to learn. It's a few books after Ephesians. Hebrews chapter seven and verse twenty-five." Mr Kemp found the place and put a finger just below it. "It's about Jesus and what he's done — and what he's doing right at this moment. Read it out, Anna."

"What, read it out loud?"

Mr. Kemp nodded.

"All right then. 'He is able to save to the uttermost those who draw near to God through him, since he always lives to make intercession for them.'"

Mr Ken looked up and caught Anna's eye. "Intercession means prayer."

"And is Jesus doing that right *now*? Praying for *us*?" Anna asked.

"Right now. He's praying for me, for you and for everyone who has trusted him to be their Saviour. You know God has an enemy, don't you? Well, this enemy is the one who keeps telling you you're not good enough. But *no one* is good enough. That's why Jesus keeps reminding God that *he* has paid for all the wrong things we've done."

Anna read it again. "Oh dear, I wish I could always remember that verse. The more I read it, the more I understand it. God seems to make some verses sort of come alive just when they're needed!" Her eyes sparkled. "I expect Jesus is saying right at this moment, 'Don't forget Anna Collins. She belongs to *me* now!'"

"Sounds like you've got a very good understanding of what it means to be a real Christian," Mr. Kemp said quietly. "And talking about verses that come alive, let me make a suggestion. Read the Gospel of John in that new Bible of yours. Maybe just a few verses each day. There are lots of promises in John's Gospel. Get a pencil and underline any verses you feel are especially for you. Then when you've finished reading the whole Gospel you can read back through the verses you've marked. And mark those verses from Ephesians and Hebrews while you're about it."

Anna liked the thought of that, but was worried about spoiling her new Bible. Mr. Kemp set her mind at rest.

"That's what Bibles are for — to be used!" he said. "Read it, mark it, and keep reading it until it's worn out. Let me know when it's worn out, and I'll buy you a new one! Don't forget to keep in touch with your Heavenly Father through prayer. Reading the Bible and praying are the ways to grow as a Christian."

Anna could have stayed talking to Matthew's dad all night, but it was time for bed. Time to start underlining those promises.

<><><>

That night was an anxious one for Matthew. Pete had phoned a couple of hours after dropping them off to say that Chip was safe, and asked what food he needed. Now Matthew lay in bed, wondering if Chip was still safe with Pete, or whether he'd managed to escape again. Perhaps Pete Morris had left the cab door open at one of his stops and forgotten all about Chip.

After breakfast he went with Anna to explore the woods. Anna told him her mum was going to invite him and his parents to stay on at the Old Barn Café for the rest of their holiday — if they didn't mind sleeping on their mattresses on the floor in the living room. Matthew said he'd love to stay if they could.

It wasn't until lunchtime that Pete drove his huge articulated truck into the park outside the transport café. There were five other trucks there, so it seemed the good news was getting around.

Matthew raced out to meet him. "Is Chip all right?"

"Chip?" Pete asked, looking puzzled. "Why, where is he?"

Matthew stood very still. Pete's face looked so serious. "Isn't he....?"

Then there was a scrabbling noise from inside the cab, followed by Chip.

Pete laughed. "That will serve you right for leaving a dog in my cab. Such a fright I got when he stood up under that rug like a great hairy monster! Now then, let's see what's for lunch. I'm very hungry indeed."

Matthew and Anna hadn't had their lunch, so they joined Pete at his table for a snack. Matthew's parents had accepted the invitation to stay on, and Mr. and Mrs. Kemp had offered to do some redecorating and helping in the café in return.

When Matthew told Pete about it, Pete said, "If you like, I'll fix up with Kate for the two of you to come back with me in the truck next time I'm passing. You can stay for a few nights. Would you like that?"

"Oh yes!" Anna said. She badly wanted to meet Kate Morris again. For one thing she wanted to find out how Kate was getting on. "I'll get Mum to come out here so you can ask her."

Pete held up a finger in caution. "Tell you what. You go and ask your ma for me. There's just something about her that...."

"Welcome back, Pete!" It was Anna's mum, wiping her hands in her apron before giving Pete a friendly hug. "Anna's been telling me a lot about you. She says you knew her father. I've been too busy in the kitchen to come out before."

"That's good, Ma," Pete said. "If you've been busy, things must be looking up."

"Yes, thanks to you. You wouldn't like to take these two out of the way for a few days, would you?"

Pete laughed. "Funny you should say that. I was just...."

Anna was deep in thought, her ears closed to the sounds of the busy transport café. She smiled to herself. A happy, deep-down smile. To think that only three days ago she'd been sitting all alone on that stone by the side of the road. So much had happened since then — to the café and to her. Was anything else exciting going to happen? It was certainly possible.

THE END

For by grace you have been saved through faith. And this is not your own doing; it is the gift of God, not a result of works, so that no one may boast (Ephesians 2:8-9).

"Yes, God loved the world so much that he gave his only Son, so that everyone who believes in him would not be lost but have eternal life" (John 3:16).

He (Jesus) is able to save to the uttermost those who draw near to God through him, since he always lives to make intercession for them (Hebrews 7:25).

About White Tree Publishing

White Tree Publishing publishes mainstream evangelical Christian literature in paperback and eBook formats, for people of all ages, by many different authors. We aim to make our eBooks available free for all eBook devices, but some distributors will only list our eBooks free at their discretion, and may make a small charge for some titles — but they are still great value!

We rely on our readers to tell their families, friends and churches about our books. Social media is a great way of doing this. Please pass the word on to Christian TV and radio networks. Also, write a positive review on the seller's/distributor's website if you are able.

The full list of our published and forthcoming Christian books is on our website

www.whitetreepublishing.com.

Please visit there regularly for updates.

Chris Wright has three grownup children, and lives in the West Country of England where he is a home group leader with his local church. More books by Chris Wright for young readers are on the next pages. His personal website is:

www.rocky-island.com

More books by Chris Wright

The Two Jays Adventure
The First Two Jays Story
Chris Wright

James and Jessica, the Two Jays, are on holiday in the West Country in England where they set out to make some exciting discoveries. Have they found the true site of an ancient holy well? Is the water in it dangerous? Why does an angry man with a bicycle tell them to keep away from the deserted stone quarry?

A serious accident on the hillside has unexpected consequences, and an old document "all in foreign" may contain a secret that's connected to the two strange stone heads in the village church — if James and Jessica can solve the puzzle. An adventure awaits!

eBook ISBN: 978-0-9954549-8-9

Paperback ISBN: 978-1-5203448-8-1
5x8 inches 196 pages
Available from major internet stores
$5.99 £4.95

The Dark Tunnel Adventure
The Second Jays Story
Chris Wright

James and Jessica, the Two Jays, are on holiday in the Derbyshire Peak District, staying near Dakedale Manor, which has been completely destroyed in a fire. Did young Sam Stirling burn his family home down? Miss Parkin, the housekeeper, says he did, and she can prove it. Sam says he didn't, but can't prove it. But Sam has gone missing. James and Jessica believe the truth lies behind one of the old iron doors inside the disused railway tunnel.

eBook ISBN: 978-0-9957594-0-4

Paperback ISBN: 978-1-5206386-3-8
5x8 inches
Available from major internet stores
$5.99 £4.95

The Cliff Edge Adventure
The Third Two Jays Story
Chris Wright

James and Jessica's Aunt Judy lives in a lonely guest house perched on top of a crumbling cliff on the west coast of Wales. She is moving out with her dog for her own safety, because she has been warned that the waves from the next big storm could bring down a large part of the cliff — and her house with it. Cousins James and Jessica, the Two Jays, are helping her sort through her possessions, and they find an old papyrus page they think could be from an ancient copy of one of the Gospels. Two people are extremely interested in having it, but can either of them be trusted? James and Jessica are alone in the house. It's dark, the electricity is off, and the worst storm in living memory is already battering the coast. *Is there someone downstairs?*

eBook ISBN: 978-0-9957594-4-2

Paperback ISBN: 9781-5-211370-3-1
$5.99 £4.95

The Midnight Farm Adventure
The Fourth Two Jays Story
Chris Wright

What is hidden in the old spoil tip by the disused Midnight Mine? Two men have permission to dig there, but they don't want anyone watching -- especially not Jessica and James, the Two Jays. And where is Granfer Joe's old tin box, full of what he called his treasure? The Easter holiday at Midnight Farm in Cornwall isn't as peaceful as

James's parents planned. An early morning bike ride nearly ends in disaster, and with the so-called Hound of the Baskervilles running loose, things turn out to be decidedly dangerous. This is the fourth Two Jays adventure story. You can read them in any order, although each one goes forward slightly in time.

eBook ISBN: 978-1-9997899-1-6

Paperback ISBN: 978-1-5497148-3-2
200 pages 5x8 inches
$5.99 £4.95

The Merlin Adventure
Chris Wright

When Daniel, Emma, Charlie and Julia, the Four Merlins, set out to sail their model boat on the old canal, strange and dangerous things start to happen. Then Daniel and Julia make a discovery they want to share with the others.

eBook ISBN: 978-0-9954549-2-7

Paperback ISBN: 9785-203447-7-5
5x8 inches 180 pages

The Seventeen Steps Adventure
Chris Wright

When Ryan's American cousin, Natalie, comes to stay with him in England, a film from their Gran's old camera holds some surprise photographs, and they discover there's more to photography than taking selfies! But where are the Seventeen Steps, and has a robbery been planned to take place there?

eBook ISBN: 978-0-9954549-7-2

Paperback ISBN: 978-1-5203448-6-7
5x8 inches 132 pages

Mary Jones and Her Bible
An Adventure Book
Chris Wright
The true story of Mary Jones's and her Bible
with a clear Christian message and optional puzzles
(Some are easy, some tricky, and some amusing)

Mary Jones saved for six years to buy a Bible of her own. In 1800, when she was 15, she thought she had saved enough, so she walked barefoot for 26 miles (more than 40km) over a mountain pass and through deep valleys in Wales to get one. That's when she discovered there were none for sale!

You can travel with Mary Jones today in this book by following clues, or just reading the story. Either way, you will get to Bala where Mary went, and if you're really quick you may be able to discover a Bible just like Mary's in the market!

The true story of Mary Jones has captured the imagination for more than 200 years. For this book, Chris Wright has looked into the old records and discovered even more of the story, which is now in this unforgettable account of Mary Jones and her Bible. Solving puzzles is part of the fun, but the whole story is in here to read and enjoy whether you try the puzzles or not. Just turn the page, and the adventure continues. It's time to get on the trail of Mary Jones!

eBook ISBN: ISBN: 978-0-9933941-5-7

Paperback ISBN 978-0-9525956-2-5
5.5 x 8.5 inches
156 pages of story, photographs, line drawings and puzzles

Pilgrim's Progress
An Adventure Book
Chris Wright

Travel with young Christian as he sets out on a difficult and perilous journey to find the King. Solve the puzzles and riddles along the way, and help Christian reach the Celestial City. Then travel with his friend Christiana. She has four young brothers who can sometimes be a bit of a problem.

Be warned, you will meet giants and lions — and even dragons! There are people who don't want Christian and Christiana to reach the city of the King and his Son. But not everyone is an enemy. There are plenty of friendly people. It's just a matter of finding them.

Are you prepared to help? Are you sure? The journey can be very dangerous! As with our book *Mary Jones and Her Bible*, you can enjoy the story even if you don't want to try the puzzles.

This is a simplified and abridged version of *Pilgrim's Progress — Special Edition*, containing illustrations and a mix of puzzles. The suggested reading age is up to perhaps ten. Older readers will find the same story told in much greater detail in *Pilgrim's Progress — Special Edition* on the next page.

eBook ISBN 13: 978-0-9933941-6-4

Paperback ISBN: 978-0-9525956-6-3
5.5 x 8.5 inches 174 pages £6.95
Available from major internet stores

Pilgrim's Progress
Special Edition
Chris Wright

This book for all ages is a great choice for young readers, as well as for families, Sunday school teachers, and anyone who wants to read John Bunyan's *Pilgrim's Progress* in a clear form.

All the old favourites are here: Christian, Christiana, the Wicket Gate, Interpreter, Hill Difficulty with the lions, the four sisters at the

House Beautiful, Vanity Fair, Giant Despair, Faithful and Talkative — and, of course, Greatheart. The list is almost endless.

The first part of the story is told by Christian himself, as he leaves the City of Destruction to reach the Celestial City, and becomes trapped in the Slough of Despond near the Wicket Gate. On his journey he will encounter lions, giants, and a creature called the Destroyer.

Christiana follows along later, and tells her own story in the second part. Not only does Christiana have to cope with her four young brothers, she worries about whether her clothes are good enough for meeting the King. Will she find the dangers in Vanity Fair that Christian found? Will she be caught by Giant Despair and imprisoned in Doubting Castle? What about the dragon with seven heads?

It's a dangerous journey, but Christian and Christiana both know that the King's Son is with them, helping them through the most difficult parts until they reach the Land of Beulah, and see the Celestial City on the other side of the Dark River. This is a story you will remember for ever, and it's about a journey you can make for yourself.

eBook ISBN: 978-0-9932760-8-8

Paperback ISBN: 978-0-9525956-7-0
5.5 x 8.5 inches 278 pages
Available from major internet stores

Agathos, The Rocky Island,
And Other Stories
Chris Wright

Once upon a time there were two favourite books for Sunday reading: *Parables from Nature* and *Agathos and The Rocky Island.*

These books contained short stories, usually with a hidden meaning. In this illustrated book is a selection of the very best of these stories, carefully retold to preserve the feel of the originals, coupled with ease of reading and understanding for today's readers.

Discover the king who sent his servants to trade in a foreign city. The butterfly who thought her eggs would hatch into baby butterflies, and the two boys who decided to explore the forbidden land beyond the castle boundary. The spider that kept being blown in the wind, the soldier who had to fight a dragon, the four children who had to find their way through a dark and dangerous forest. These are just six of the nine stories in this collection. Oh, and there's also one about a rocky island!

This is a book for a young person to read alone, a family or parent to read aloud, Sunday school teachers to read to the class, and even for grownups who want to dip into the fascinating stories of the past all by themselves. Can you discover the hidden meanings? You don't have to wait until Sunday before starting!

eBook ISBN: 978-0-9927642-7-2

Paperback ISBN: 978-0-9525956-8-7
5.5 x 8.5 inches 148 pages £5.95
Available from major internet stores

Zephan and the Vision
Chris Wright

An exciting story about the adventures of two angels who seem to know almost nothing – until they have a vision!

Two ordinary angels are caring for the distant Planet Eltor, and they are about to get a big shock – they are due to take a trip to Planet Earth! This is Zephan's story of the vision he is given before being allowed to travel with Talora, his companion angel, to help two young people fight against the enemy.

Arriving on Earth, they discover that everyone lives in a small castle. Some castles are strong and built in good positions, while others appear weak and open to attack. But it seems that the best-looking castles are not always the most secure.

Meet Castle Nadia and Castle Max, the two castles that Zephan and Talora have to defend. And meet the nasty creatures who have built shelters for themselves around the back of these castles. And worst of all, meet the shadow angels who live in a cave on Shadow Hill. This is a story about the forces of good and the forces of evil. Who will win the battle for Castle Nadia?

The events in this story are based very loosely on John Bunyan's allegory *The Holy War*.

E-book ISBN: 978-0-9932760-6-4

Paperback ISBN: 978-0-9525956-9-4
5.5 x 8.5 inches 216 pages
Available from major internet stores

Two of four short books of help in the Christian life by Chris Wright:

Starting Out – help for new Christians of all ages. Paperback ISBN 978-1-4839-622-0-7, eBook ISBN: 978-0-9933941-0-2

Running Through the Bible – a simple understanding of what's in the Bible – Paperback ISBN: 978-0-9927642-6-5, eBook ISBN: 978-0-9933941-3-3

So, What Is a Christian? An introduction to a personal faith. Paperback ISBN: 978-0-9927642-2-7, eBook ISBN: 978-0-9933941-2-6

Help! – Explores some problems we can encounter with our faith. Paperback ISBN 978-0-9927642-2-7, eBook ISBN: 978-0-9933941-1-9

Printed in Great Britain
by Amazon